LIFE
ON HOLD

D1495357

Karen McQuestion

LIFE ON HOLD

SKYSCAPE

SKYSCAPE

Text copyright ©2010 Karen McQuestion
All rights reserved
Printed in the United States of America

This book was self published, in a slightly different form, in 2009.

Published by Amazon Publishing
Attn: Amazon Children's Publishing
P.O. Box 400818
Las Vegas, NV 89140

ISBN-13: 1935597272
ISBN-10: 9781935597278

For my daughter, Maria who insists that teenagers' bonfires aren't at all the way I imagine them to be

Acknowledgments

Terry Goodman always gets top billing when it comes to my gratitude. He once sent me an e-mail that changed my life for the better, and I'll never forget it. He's smart, funny, and diplomatic, and I feel fortunate to work with him.

Sarah Tomashek has incredible people skills and great marketing strategies, and I've benefitted from both. I'm lucky to have her on my side.

This is my fifth book with AmazonEncore, and I couldn't be happier. Thanks to Sarah Gelman, Victoria Griffith, Jessica R. Smith, Jennifer Williams, and the behind-the-scenes team for their hard work on my behalf.

I am indebted to foreign rights agent Taryn Fagerness for her diligence and enthusiasm.

The following people gave me helpful feedback on the book in its earliest form: Cherie Bussert, Jessica Coats, Kathleen Coats, Vickie Coats, Kay Ehlers, Geri Erickson, Shawnee Griffin, Alice L. Kent, Felicity Librie, Maria McQuestion, Jeannée Sacken, Shelly Tenwinkel, and Robert Vaughan. Thanks to all! I really appreciate it.

Thank you to the Hartland Public Library for providing me with a comfortable writing chair and a stress-free environment.

I've been remiss in the past for not mentioning the ones who started me off on my publishing journey. I'd like to thank the Kindle readers, especially the ones on the Amazon message boards and Kindleboards.com. My good fortune is directly connected to their willingness to give an unknown author a chance back when I first self-published my books on Kindle. Their reviews and recommendations led me to where I am today. Believe me when I say I'm truly grateful.

My family means the world to me. I am blessed to be the mother of Jack, Maria, and Charlie. They are good people, and oh so smart. Plus, they make me laugh on a regular basis.

And saving the best for last: thank you to my husband, Greg, for everything.

Chapter 1
Paranoid Girl

At the end of a long, hard day, all I wanted was to go home. It sounds easy enough, and it would have been, if not for Dorothy, the most annoying crossing guard on the planet. She was really there for the younger kids, but she insisted on helping everyone across the street, holding up her sign even if there weren't any cars in sight. She prided herself on knowing everyone's name, and I was a problem for her because I wouldn't tell her mine.

The first time Dorothy asked my name, she caught me on a bad day. I smiled and said I preferred to be anonymous. The way I saw it, she didn't need to know—I was a sophomore in high school, not a third grader. When she brought it up again the next day, I told her I was pleading the Fifth, which seemed to confuse her. She tried to guess. Amanda? Stephanie? For days she greeted me with different names. Rachel? Krista? It got old real fast. Later she tried compliments, telling me that a pretty girl like me should wear bright colors and not just black all the time. Occasionally she offered me candy, saying we were celebrating Happy Thursday or some crap like that. After a while I wanted to tell her my name, just to put an end to the game, but it seemed awkward to just say it, like I'd been holding out for nothing. By the end of September, I started going around her intersection. It seemed to be the only way out.

Avoiding the crossing guard's intersection made my walk a little longer and meant I went right by the kids' insane asylum. Technically it was called the Mental Health Unit for Children and Adolescents, MHUCA for short, but I always liked to think of it as Mother HUCA. It was a huge red building, flat on every side including the roof so it looked like an enormous brick. The patio in the back of the building, which is what I passed, was a squarish piece of concrete surrounded by scraggly looking grass, all of it closed in by a chain-link fence.

My walk home came at the same time as some kind of break the crazy kids got. Every time I went past they were there—a dozen or so skeezy kids my age, clustered by the back door like smokers outside of a mall. At first I thought they *were* smoking. They had that hungry, antsy look like they desperately needed something. They stared at the ground even as they talked amongst themselves. I noticed the girl with the long, dark hair right away because she always stood about ten feet away from them, like she was making a statement. I'm not part of *that* group, was my take on it. She fidgeted and kept looking back and forth, like she was afraid someone was going to catch her doing something wrong. Paranoid Girl, I named her.

One day I found myself slowing down to watch. I wondered what these kids had done to get committed to a residential treatment center. I scanned their faces looking for clues, but you couldn't tell by sight what their problems were. Just as well, I guess.

I knew I shouldn't stare, but they fascinated me. I paused and put my backpack on the ground, pretending to look for something inside the front compartment. At school I'd stopped using my locker because it was nowhere near my classes, and now I had to carry my books with me all the time. One time, just for the hell of it, I weighed my backpack on my bathroom scale. Thirty-one pounds. Thirty-one pounds of boring-ass textbooks wrecking my back.

Paranoid Girl saw me stop and got a panicked look on her face. She glanced nervously at the building and back at me, like she was a spy in a movie and I was about to give away her identity. She held out a hand and shooed me away, actually shooed me away, like she had some kind of control over a stranger on the sidewalk twenty feet away.

I pointed to myself in an exaggerated gesture. *Who, me?* She nodded yes and made that little gesture again, her hand a swinging door, and then she looked nervously at the group of crazy kids still hunched over in their football huddle.

I wasn't in the mood to follow orders from a stranger behind a fence. Just to make a point, I waved at Paranoid Girl, a big straight-arm wave, like I was trying to get her attention from across a parking lot. Mentally I sent her a message: *See? I'm not going anywhere until I feel like it.*

She shook her head no and jabbed a thumb toward the group of crazy kids. Seeing her expression made me wonder what was up. She looked so worried.

If I could have given Paranoid Girl some advice, I would have told her to just let it go. Just do whatever it takes to get through the day—that was how I played it, and it worked for me. I got my work done at school and kept a low profile out in the world. Mostly, I waited for it to be over. I actually had a notebook where I diagramed a calendar of the next two and a quarter years. A countdown to my eighteenth birthday and freedom. At the end of each day I took a Sharpie marker and X-ed off that day's square. It gave me a sense of satisfaction to think I was another day closer.

I waved to Paranoid Girl again, mentally sending out my attitude. Just let it all go, I thought. Whatever it is, it's not worth it. She shook her head, and her whole body shuddered. She didn't seem to get it.

I zipped up my backpack and gave her a smile. It was then that the group of skeezy kids noticed me. They lifted their heads like dogs smelling meat, and one of the boys, a big hulk in a camo jacket, yelled, "Hey, what are you looking at?" As if on cue, they all left their spot by the back door and started moving toward me. As they picked up speed, they started yelling. "You have a staring problem?" a girl in dreadlocks called out, her arm thrust in an accusatory point. Another guy yelled, "Get lost, bitch."

It happened so fast, really fast, and I frantically zipped my backpack shut and hoisted it over my shoulder. They were heading straight for me, running now. They didn't slow down when they got to the fence, just slammed into it. *Bam.* The fence had some give to it and stretched a little in my direction. The kids in back smashed against the ones in front. Their faces contorted against the chain-link, and they started screaming profanities that, just for the record, did not describe me. My flight reflex kicked in as they hit the fence, and I took off—not running, because of the backpack, but walking as fast as I could. When I got to the corner, I looked behind me to see them all wandering back to the building. Paranoid Girl, still in her same spot, caught my eye and raised her hands, palms up, and shrugged—*I tried to tell you.*

Chapter 2

New Girl

"Hi, I'm Rae. I'm new here."

I've said those words more times than I can count. My mom and I move a lot, and this is my usual introduction at school and in the neighborhood. After I've said it, I know someone will take pity and show me around, usually one of those girls who likes to take charge of situations. I adapt well, so I fit in anywhere, but I don't dig in too deep because we never stay longer than a year or so.

If I've learned anything it's to not get too attached. Maybe that's why I didn't want to tell the crossing guard my name. Leaving is painful, and the more people there are to miss, the worse it is. One time in particular I *did* get too attached. It was in middle school when this girl, Chelsea, tried to give me half of her necklace—one of those ones that look like half a heart with the word "Best" on one half and "Friend" on the other. I told her my mother wouldn't let me keep it, which was a lie because Gina never stopped me from doing anything.

Even though I didn't take the necklace, Chelsea and I got to be close. So close that I told her everything—how I didn't know my own father's name and that Gina used to smoke pot and how

I felt about moving all the time, which is that I hated it, but I went along with it. I told Chels about the one time I strongly objected, when my mother had a meltdown, crying and carrying on about everything she gave up in life by having me as a teenager. It was hard to raise a baby by herself, but she did it, is what Mom said. She stayed up nights with a crying baby while her friends were out partying and she didn't complain. She sacrificed a lot, and that was fine, but wasn't she entitled to live her life and do what she wanted now that I was older and things were easier? By this point I started feeling really guilty.

The conversation had shifted from there. Mom said, "And don't we have fun together? Aren't we closer than most mothers and daughters?" I had to admit we were. Then she went on about how the new place would be so much better: a fresh start, an adventure. And she said I shouldn't let fear of new places hold me back, that change was a good thing. By the time she finished campaigning I felt really bad for standing in her way, and I cracked. I said okay to the move, even though I didn't want to go.

Chelsea was the only person I ever told all my secrets to, and when my mom and I moved five hundred miles away from her, I felt like my heart was torn out of me. We tried to stay in touch with phone calls and IM-ing, but it wasn't the same. And after that I heard from Chelsea's new best friend (she didn't even *like* this girl when I lived there) that Chelsea told her all about me not having a father on my birth certificate, something she swore she would never ever tell. So much for promises. Ever since then I've had a no-best-friends policy, and I've stuck to it. My mom is number one on my cell phone speed dial, sadly enough. I'm not on MySpace of Facebook, but if I were I'd have a problem picking someone for my number-one space. Best friends are for other people.

So I don't have best friends. What I have are people—not really good friends, but a notch up from acquaintances. Here at Whitman High School I have two people, a funny Japanese guy named Mason Mihashi, and Kylie Johnson, an undersized girl. And I mean *seriously* undersized. I'm on the short side and Mason's not much taller, but she's technically a midget or dwarf or something. I never really asked. The victim of a malfunctioning pituitary gland, I heard her say once.

Everybody's got something.

Mason, Kylie, and I eat lunch together, say hi in the halls, and once in a while see a movie or go to a football game. Two people. That's really all I need. At some of my schools I didn't even have that. And Mason and Kylie are good. Better than most, I'd say. Mason has a wicked sense of humor, and Kylie *gets* people faster than me even. She can read them instantly. I think she has a future as a psychiatrist or a parole officer. Nothing gets past her.

My mother thinks I make friends easily, but that's not true. What I actually do is connect with other kids who aren't in a group either. The loose ends. At Glenview High School my people were named Elizabeth and Latonya. Before that, at Washington Heights High, I had Russ. Just Russ. He was pretty cool with his "stick it to the man" attitude and counterculture views, but kind of depressed most of the time.

I tried to keep a diary once to list all the places we'd lived and all the "friends" I've had, but I didn't stay with it, and then it got lost in one of our moves. So now I just have the notebook I mentioned before, the one where I keep track of the countdown to my eighteenth birthday. I hate not having a say in my own life. Sometimes my mom acts like she's giving me choices, but she's really not. There's not much I can do about it.

In this same notebook I also put information about my dad, the mystery man I know nothing about. Every time my mom mentions something about him I write it down. Most of it isn't true—I know because she keeps contradicting herself. I write it all down anyway because you never know. There might be a seed of truth in there somewhere. Mom says when I'm an adult she'll tell me the whole story, and she's pretty firm on that timeline. Another reason to look forward to my eighteenth birthday.

Chapter 3
Watch Your Step

One school day in October, as I sat down to eat lunch with Mason and Kylie, I heard the usual roar of Blake Daly *arriving*. He does this thing when he walks in the door of the cafeteria—he calls out something like "Booya!" or "Incoming!" and all of the Blake Juniors and other wannabes who are already sitting at his table (he comes in late just so he can make an entrance) yell it back like it's a tribal war chant instead of some made-up bullshit from an attention-seeking jock. Today Blake yelled out, "Oh yeah," and predictably, his band of groupies bellowed, "Oh yeah!" like they were at a rock concert or something. Besides being annoying, this whole routine is incredibly unfair. If anyone else did it, they'd get a detention for being disruptive, but not Blake. Obviously the rules don't apply to everyone.

I kept my attention on my sandwich during the Blake drama, although I was aware of him going through the lunch line and laughing a little too loudly at something the lunch lady told him. He always acted nice to the teachers and cafeteria workers, but made fun of them behind their backs. I'd encountered Blakes at other schools. I knew their ways, how they had to be the center of everything, the disdain they had for most other people. Blake had no idea what a stereotype he was. Every high school in the country had their own top dogs, all of them completely oblivious to the fact that they wouldn't be anything special once they got out in the big world. I had a sudden amusing thought that a good idea for a movie would be to fill a stadium with every Blake-type kid from every high school in America and make them compete against each other. I was a little fuzzy on what kind of competition I'd have them do. Some sort of fight-to-the-death thing. I'd have to think about it and fill that part in later.

I looked up in time to see Kylie grinning at me across the table. She peeled the top off her yogurt and laughed. Mason sat next to her looking like he was about to crack up too. Something was funny.

"What?"

"We've been watching you for the last ten minutes, and I've been waving at you."

Mason smiled so widely I could see his canines. Man, he had white teeth. "When you get lost in thought, you're in another world," he said.

I looked at them in mock indignation. "What's your point?"

Kylie shrugged and gestured with her spoon. "You just look so cute. Did you know you have a vein in your forehead that sticks out when you concentrate really hard?"

"No way." I reached up to touch my forehead. Smooth, just like I remembered.

"Of course it's not doing it *now*," Mason said. "Only when you're doing your heavy thinking."

"How much does it stick out?" I asked, concerned. One more thing to be self-conscious about.

"Like this," Mason said, putting his finger against his forehead. "Only not a finger."

"It's not *that* obvious," Kylie said. "Don't let him get to you."

The subject of my forehead distracted us from the rest of the lunch-hour noise—the talking and laughing and banging that filled the room. We were in our own world, with Mason going on about blood flow and what causes veins to protrude, and Kylie assuring me that lots of people had the forehead vein thing and that it really wasn't that noticeable.

We were so into the conversation that we didn't even see Blake coming up alongside us. I only noticed him when he fell flat on his back next to our table. One moment he was upright, sauntering along with his tray in front of him like he ruled the school. A split second later he was down on the floor. His tray went up as he fell; an apple catapulted upward as the rest of his food slid downward. In the quickest show of reflexes I've ever seen in my life, Mason reached out and grabbed the apple as it came back down. The whole thing happened in an instant. In shocked silence, I burst out laughing.

Blake sat up stunned, his legs sticking out in front of him. He still held onto the tray, but his pizza slice had landed upside down on his lap. Mason jumped up and extended a hand to help him up. "Dude, you okay?"

"No, I'm not okay." He was turning red now and looked really pissed off. "Some dumbass spilled something and made me slip." He glared at me, like it was my fault.

The look on his face struck me as really funny. The more I tried to stop laughing the worse it got, and now some of the other kids at surrounding tables were laughing too, a few of them clapping and calling out things like, "Way to go, Blake!"

"I'm sorry," I said, wiping my eyes. "But the way you went down and then the apple went up…" A person really had to see it to get the full picture. He'd gone down fast, and then the apple had flown upward like it was a whole separate thing, as if it had a life of its own. Then Mason's hand shooting out and catching it. All so perfect, it could have been a scene in a movie.

"It's not funny." Blake swatted Mason's hand away. I guess he didn't want any help getting up. He stood up slowly and brushed off the front of his legs, but his pizza slice had left a tomato sauce smear on his khakis right over his crotch. "Great, just great." He gave me the evil eye, and I tried again to hold back my laughter.

"I really am sorry," I said. "It just struck me as funny. Sorry about your pants." I tried to hold back my laughter, but I was so far gone I was choking on it.

His face contorting in anger, he took a step toward me like he was going to get in my face, and I reached toward my backpack for the pepper spray I always carried. My mom had bought it for me when I got my first period, like suddenly men would be attacking me. I'd put it in the small front pocket, like she'd suggested, but I'd never used it. She told me when my gut was afraid I shouldn't hesitate.

"Hey," Mason yelled. "Back off." He stepped in between me and Blake, which was hugely courageous because Blake was about eight inches and fifty pounds bigger than him.

"Out of my way, chink-boy."

His voice was threatening, but Mason didn't movie. "I'm Japanese, not Chinese, you moron." I noticed Mason's hand, still holding the apple, rise up a few inches.

"Chinese, Japanese, whatever. It doesn't make a difference," Blake screamed, his vocal cords jutting out of his throat. I think he meant to come off like he was tough, but he sounded like an idiot.

By now three of Blake's guys were clustered behind him. One of them, Nick Dunstan, whooped and clapped a hand on Blake's shoulder. "It does make a difference, Blake. They're completely different countries."

Blake glared at him, but Nick's gaze was on me, a big grin on his face like we were in on some secret. But if there was a secret between us, someone forgot to tell me.

Mr. Meltzer, the lunchroom supervisor, walked toward us with his keys jangling. "What's the problem here?" As usual, he'd waited until a group had gathered. He only responded to situations that were impossible to ignore.

"Blake hit a wet spot," Kylie said, taking another spoonful of yogurt. "He fell down." She gave me a sly smile.

"Are you hurt, son?" Mr. Meltzer put his hand on Blake's arm. Big mistake.

Angrily, Blake shook him off. "I'm fine."

Nick picked up the tray and the slice of pizza. Another guy retrieved a Gatorade from underneath a neighboring table. Nick held up the pizza, which drooped like a clock in a Salvador Dali painting. "You want me to get you another piece?" he asked, but Blake was already heading out the door of the lunchroom. Off to the bathroom, was my guess, but I had news for him—that blob of pizza sauce wasn't going away easily.

"Okay, people," Meltzer said. "Back to your seats. I'll get someone to clean this up." Everyone was pretty much drifting back to their tables anyway, so his big display of authority didn't count for much.

Mason took his seat. "That was interesting."

"Thanks for sticking up for me," I said. "No one ever did that for me before."

"No problem. Anything for a friend." He waved a hand and took a bite out of Blake's apple.

I watched Blake's crew as they headed back to their table. A whole herd of them. As if he could feel my eyes on his back, Nick stopped and turned around so he was facing my table. He caught my eye, picked up the droopy pizza, and pretended he was going to take a bite. I wasn't sure what that was all about, but he made me smile.

"What are you looking at?" Kylie asked.

"That Nick Dunstan. He's goofing around with Blake's pizza." Kylie swiveled around, but he'd already turned to join the others. "What's his story, anyway?" I asked.

"What do you mean?" She studied my face.

"I mean, what's the deal with him being in Blake's group? He doesn't seem like the rest of them." Most of the guys at Blake's table looked like athletes, or football players anyway, but Nick didn't have the same build. He wasn't big or muscular, just sort of lanky and thin. He had to be the water boy or team manager or something.

"He's going out with Crystal Palmer, and she's part of that group. He's in by association," Kylie said. She got a sudden smug look on her face. "You think he's cute, don't you?" She nudged Mason. "Our girl has a crush on one of Blakey's boys."

"I do not," I protested. "I just think he's interesting. He doesn't fit."

Mason leaned across the table and started singing. "Rae and Nicky sitting in a tree. K-I-S-S-I-N-G…"

"Stop it," I said, reaching over to cover his mouth. "You are so immature." Trust Mason to torment me like a fourth grader.

Underneath my hand, he finished a muffled version of the verse. "First comes love, then comes marriage…"

Chapter 4
Message from the Smedster

When I got home to our apartment, Gina and her friend Carla were in the kitchen smoking cigarettes and drinking Diet Coke, flipping through the newest issues of *Elle* and *Glamour*.

My mother could justify spending money on makeup and magazines and hair products because she was in the fashion business. Or at least that's what she thought. In reality she was a nail technician, which is just a sideways way of saying she was a manicurist. It's not anything I'd want to do, but Gina is extremely good at it. First off, she has people skills like you wouldn't believe. It's impossible not to like her, and believe me, I've tried. She loves to talk, and she's good at listening. She notices everything and gives compliments the way other people exhale. Every time we move she gets a job no problem, and within months she's the one all the customers want. When I was little I loved to count her tips. I made a game of smoothing out the bills and stacking the coins by size. I used to think we were rich.

Not only is Gina a people person, but she's also an artist. The only difference between her and the painters in art galleries is that her canvases are fingernails. I swear she could do full-size paintings if she had the interest. Every year for my birthday she creates a banner that's absolutely beautiful. I have last year's rolled up in my closet. I would have kept all of them, but Gina believes in traveling light and not hanging onto a lot of crap.

"Hey babe," Gina said when I came into the room. "How was school?" She gave me a wide smile, the same one she greeted me with every day. A so-glad-to-see-you grin. You'd think I'd been away forever or something.

"Good." I shook off my backpack and set it against the wall. "I got an A on my English test and a B plus on my biology quiz. We have to dissect a frog tomorrow."

"Yuck," Gina said, making a face like she'd tasted something nasty. "You want me to write a note so you can get out of it? We could say it's against our religion or something."

"No," I said and went into the fridge for a bottle of water. "I don't mind. I'm doing it with my lab partner. We did a worm last week and it was pretty interesting."

"That's my girl," Gina said to Carla. "Did I tell you she got a 3.8 average last year?"

"You did tell me." Carla nodded. "Smart girl." She was a new friend to my mom. Gina made friends very easily, mostly from work.

I sat down across from the two of them and unscrewed the cap from my bottle.

"And look at her with the water," Gina said, pointing. "She stopped drinking soda in seventh grade. Rae's a better person than me. I'm not sure how that happened."

"Maybe from her father's side?" Carla said, not knowing, of course, that the topic of my father was off limits.

"I wouldn't know about that," I said. "My father is an un-known. I might not even have one for all I know."

Gina frowned. "Give it a rest, Rae. I told you everything you need to know." She snuffed out her cigarette in the ashtray she'd stolen from the Hard Rock Café. "By the way," she said, conveniently changing the subject, "your vice principal called this afternoon."

"Mr. Smedley?"

Gina nodded. "That's the one."

This couldn't be good. Mr. Smedley was in charge of discipline. Mason called him the Smedster and did a wicked impression of him, complete with the exaggerated way he pushed his glasses up the bridge of his nose. As for me, I just tried to stay out of Mr. Smedley's way. Usually I saw him in the hall yelling out, "Move it along, people. Enough with the screwing around." I once witnessed a scuffle near the water fountain, or "bubbler" as they insisted on calling it here in Wisconsin. Some kid got his face pushed into it as he was taking a drink, and the Smedster came out of nowhere to haul the offender off to his office. He was tough.

"Don't look so worried," Gina said, putting a cigarette in her mouth and flicking a lighter so that a blue-gold flame shot out of the top. She inhaled and set the lighter down on the table. "You're not in any trouble. I asked. He said he wants to ask a favor of you."

"A favor of *me*?"

She exhaled, the smoke coming out in a hazy wisp. "That's what he said. You're supposed to go to his office fifteen minutes before school starts."

"Did he say what the favor was?" I pulled at the edge of the label on my Aquafina and tore one lone thin piece from around the top.

"Nope, but he did say you've been a model student. You're not in any trouble."

Yeah, because the Smedster always called students in just to chat. I wondered if he wanted me to tell on someone else. I really didn't have any information that anyone else didn't have. And how did he even know who I was? Out of hundreds of kids in that school he wanted me to do him a favor? Something wasn't adding up.

Gina laughed. "Chill, Rae. I'm sure it's nothing. If they give you any grief at that school, you can always switch and go somewhere else. Hey!" She snapped her fingers. "Maybe you could homeschool. We could order that curriculum in a box off the Internet and you could work from here. Admit it," she said, pointing my way, "that's an interesting idea."

"Interesting, yes," I said. Homeschooling? What was she thinking? All I could envision were those religious families, the ones with the little girls wearing Amish dresses and the boys with their slicked-back hair and matching polo shirts. I'd seen groups of them at the mall, following their mother single file, pretending it was a field trip. Of course, in Gina's version of homeschooling, I'd be sitting at the kitchen table filling out worksheets while she came and went from the salon, depending on her schedule. I'd keep her company while she read her horoscope and answered her cell phone. Bleah. No thank you, I'd rather go to a real high school, one that would get me into college. I picked up my backpack and slung it over one shoulder. "If you'll excuse me, I think I'll go to my room and start my homework."

"Nice seeing you, hon," Carla said, giving me a wave like a salute.

"Nice seeing you too, Carla."

From the hallway I heard Carla say, "You sure did luck out with that girl."

And my mom answered, "Isn't she something? I've never had a bit of trouble with her."

Yes, No Trouble Rae, that would be me.

Chapter 5
The Rae Maddox
Integration Program

I've always been uncomfortable around men, especially authority figures. My mom, on the other hand, has never had a problem talking to anyone, especially men. It doesn't hurt that Gina's very pretty. She has red hair, curly red hair—the kind that stands out even at a distance. About once a month, she puts some kind of rinse on it that "enhances" the color, but she's a true redhead from birth. She's also petite and thin, but not in a skinny, anorexic model kind of way. More like a movie star from the 1920s, the ones with the big eyes and heart-shaped faces.

She's dated a lot of men over the years, and I can always tell how surprised they are when they meet me, the daughter with the straight brown hair and ripped blue jeans. The funny thing is, Gina thinks I look great. She likes my ripped jeans and black T-shirts, my silver hoop earrings. She respects that I have my own style.

Gina would have had no problem walking in the Smedster's office that next morning. She thinks the world loves her, and it usually does. I, however, know the world doesn't care about me one way or the other, so I'm always cautious.

I got to school early and walked into the office. I couldn't shake a feeling of dread. The head secretary, a large woman with a pencil tucked behind her ear, was already there tapping away on her computer. "Can I help you, dear?" For some reason, her kind voice made me feel a bit better.

I cleared my throat and leaned on the counter that separated us. "Mr. Smedley left a message with my mom asking me to come in and see him before school."

She stood up from her desk and gave me a hard look over her wire-rimmed glasses. "You would be Rae, then?"

I nodded. It was bad when they knew your name.

"The other girl is already there, and Mr. Smedley should be arriving any minute. You can either wait here or in his office." She indicated a short hallway off to the right.

"The other girl?" There were two of us? Could the other girl be Kylie? I doubted it. I would have heard if Smedley had called her house. This whole thing was so confusing. Gina had said I wasn't in any trouble, so why did I have this uneasy feeling like something bad was going to happen?

"Go on down then," the woman encouraged, like I was a little kid or something. "You two can talk until he gets here." She pointed. "First door on the left."

As promised, there was another girl in Mr. Smedley's office, but I'd never seen her before. She sat at a small circular table just inside the doorway, not much bigger than the kind they had in preschool. Four molded plastic chairs were arranged around it at perfectly spaced intervals. Mr. Smedley's desk was on the opposite wall. To give him credit, at least his office didn't have any of those inspirational posters—the kind with the kitten dangling from a branch headed by the words "Just Hang in There." Instead he had framed photos of sailboats with sunsets in the background.

Or maybe they were sunrises—hard to say, because in a photo it looks the same.

The girl at the table was reading a paperback book. She ignored my entrance, which gave me a chance to look at her. Her long, dark hair was pulled back in a French braid, and she was wearing what my grandmother would describe as a blouse, with a beige cable-knit sweater vest over it, and a pair of black pants with a crease down the front of each leg. The perfect look for a job interview. Not so good for high school.

I put my backpack on the floor, pulled up a chair, and sat down, tucking my legs underneath. There was a moment of awkward silence—awkward for me, but not for her, since she didn't even seem to notice my existence. I debated joking about me being invisible or trying something lame like, "That must be a really good book," but I finally settled on a traditional greeting. "Hi," I said. "I'm Rae."

She lifted her head from the pages. Her eyes were an odd shade of green; I immediately thought *colored contact lenses*. Her hair was an inky black, but not dyed like the goth girls. Based on her eyebrows I thought it was pretty close to her natural coloring. She sighed and then turned toward me. "Are we starting already? Because I thought I had until Smedley got here."

"What's this all about?" I shifted in my seat. No one had comfort in mind when these chairs were designed. They were clearly meant for people who'd violated the rules and had come to this office to find out their punishment. "Why are we here?"

"I'm new, you're not. You're going to show me around the school and tell me what's what." She sounded bored.

"But who are you?" It was hard not to sound irritated. Showing someone around was supposed to be a voluntary activity. Let the girls from the Key Club do it—they lived for this crap. Not to mention the fact that I was new this year myself. I barely knew my own way around. If it weren't for the fact that I'd talked to Kylie in current events back on my first day, I'd still be eating lunch alone. Good old always-friendly Kylie, the complete opposite of this girl, who now stared at me blankly. I tried again and said, "I don't think I caught your name." Mentally I came up with a few of my own: French Braid Girl, Fake Eye Color Girl, or maybe Stuck-Up Bitch Girl.

As it turned out, none of my guesses were right. "My name is Allison," she said, closing her book just as Mr. Smedley walked into the room.

"Good morning!" he said brightly, hanging his jacket on a hook on the back of the door. "Both of you girls were so early, you made me look bad." He laughed like he'd made a joke. I gave him a pity smile, but Allison didn't react at all.

He turned to us and clasped his hands together. "I assume you've had a chance to talk?"

"Not really," I said. "I told her my name, she told me hers."

"I said I was new." Allison flipped her braid around so it hung over one shoulder. Again she sounded bored, disinterested.

"That's a start," the Smedster said, sitting down on the chair next to me. "What it comes down to is this: we have recently devised a program for integrating new students into our curriculum, Rae. It's brand-new, sort of a pilot program if you will, and you've been chosen to play an important role in implementing it here at Whitman High School."

He smiled like this was good news, like I was getting some sort of award or recognition instead of getting dumped on. My heart took a dive. I didn't want to play an important role, didn't want to take part in their pilot program. All I wanted was to keep doing what I'd always done—go to school, blend in, go home, do my homework, talk to Gina, check off another day in my notebook, and go to bed. Lather, rinse, repeat, over and over again until I was eighteen and could put it all behind me and start living my own life.

Mr. Smedley said, "So what do you think of that, Rae? You'll get to be Allison's introduction to Whitman High, and be in on the ground floor of a brand-new program. If it works out, all the other high schools in the area will follow suit."

"I don't know if I'm the best person for this pilot program," I said, mentally scrambling for a way to get out of this. "I'm new here myself, and don't know that much about the school." I leaned toward him and looked him right in the eye. It was a trick I'd learned from Gina. "It's not that I don't want to help out. It's just that I don't think having me as a guide would be giving Allison the *best* introduction to Whitman. I'm sure there are lots of students who could do a better job. I wouldn't want to shortchange Allison." I sat back, satisfied. I'd given a calm, convincing argument and phrased it in such a way that I sounded more concerned for the welfare of others than for myself. "One of the members of the Key Club, perhaps?"

He shook his head. "Sorry, Rae. I see your point, but I feel very confident in saying that you are just the person to be Allison's guide. You were chosen for very specific reasons." He began to tick off the reasons on his fingers. "You're taking the same classes Allison needs to take this semester. Your teachers all rave about your work—they say you're very mature for your age. As a new student yourself, you've assimilated beautifully. You're respected by your peers. I could go on and on, but the long and short of it is that it's already set up." He leaned over and looked me straight in the eye. Damn! He knew Gina's trick too. "I know I'm throwing this at you without much notice, but on behalf of the administration here, we do appreciate it."

I knew when I'd lost a battle. "What exactly do I have to do?" I looked at Allison. Her face didn't give anything away. I was betting she wasn't any more thrilled about this program than I was.

Mr. Smedley's face took on a triumphant look. "This is going to be so easy. Just do what you usually do, but include Allison. Follow your schedule, show her around the school, introduce her to your friends. Maybe find a place for her at your lunch table. This isn't rocket science, Rae. It's just one human being helping another human being. That's the beauty of the program. Who knows, maybe we'll wind up naming this program after you—The Rae Maddox Integration Program." He laughed merrily.

"That's okay. No need for that." There was no way I wanted my name connected to this. Generations of kids would hate me by association.

Allison spoke up. "So I have the exact same schedule as Rae?" Maybe it was my imagination, but she looked relieved.

"All except for third hour when you have different math classes." He got up, pulled a sheet of paper off his desk, and handed it to Allison. "But don't worry, you're just across the hall from her, so you can still walk together." As if he'd timed it, the first bell rang then. "There's your cue, girls. I better let you go, so you won't be late."

We all stood up at the same time, our chairs scraping against the linoleum. As we walked out of his office, he said, "Thanks, Rae. And Allison?" She stopped to look back. "Don't forget my offer. If you need anything, my door is always open."

Chapter 6
Relatively Rude

That morning was excruciatingly long. Allison stayed by my side like a dog trained to heel. She moved right along next to me, so close our elbows were almost touching, but that wasn't the annoying part. The annoying part was that she wouldn't answer any of my questions. In fact, most of the time she seemed to be ignoring me. I tried to make small talk, honestly I did.

Our conversations in the hallway went like this:

Me: Just our luck we get picked for this pilot program, huh?

Her: (complete silence, a slight nod)

Me: So, did you move here, or are you just transferring schools?

Her: I'm new.

Me: I can't believe Mr. Smedley said his door is always open to you. When I started at the beginning of the school year, I got my schedule like everyone else and they just set me loose. They're really giving you the special treatment. What's that all about?

Her: Hmmm.

I introduced her to our teachers, which seemed to startle them. They weren't expecting a new student, much less one dressed like a librarian. Allison didn't have a backpack or any school supplies, just a purse, a large patent leather purse so shiny you could see your face in it.

In each class we stood at the front of the room while the other students found their seats. Allison mutely pulled her schedule out of her purse to prove to the teacher she was supposed to be there, and let me do the talking. I felt like I was one of those assistants who follow the special ed kids from class to class. Being in charge of someone else was exhausting. Not to mention that it put me in the spotlight, something I'd tried to avoid my entire life. Frankly, Allison was a drag.

And the worst part of it was that she seemed to resent me, or look down on me or something. Like she was embarrassed to be seen with me, which was odd because she was the one who didn't fit in. Me, I blended, I really did. In fact, I blended so well I doubt if many sophomores besides Mason and Kylie even knew my name.

Third hour Allison had geometry and I had algebra, so we had to part ways. Thank God. I wondered how many days before I could cut her loose, say I was going to my locker and I'd meet up with her later. It would be hard, given that our schedules had the same flight pattern, but maybe I could work something out. Best-case scenario: Allison makes friends with the student council clan, and I'm off the hook completely. I made a mental note to stop by Mr. Smedley's office after school to find out how long I was obligated to do this. There had to be some limit.

By lunchtime I felt like I did when I'd babysat one too many hours. Allison seemed oblivious to my feelings and kept pace with me down the hallway as I headed to the cafeteria. Her silence made me nervous, and I found myself chattering as we walked. I pointed out the bathrooms to avoid and the hallway that led to nowhere but a locked closet. I also explained the layout of the school, how the classrooms were numbered odd and even on alternating sides of the hallway. Through all of it she said nothing. She didn't even acknowledge she heard me, which was kind of rude. At least, though, I could tell Mr. Smedley I'd done my part. No one could say I hadn't shown her around.

At the doorway of the cafeteria I said, "I'm not buying food. I always bring my lunch." I held up my backpack to indicate I had it with me. "If you want to go ahead..." I gestured toward the line.

"No thanks, I'll go with you." It was the longest string of words I'd heard from her since we'd left the principal's office.

"Okay, have it your way."

We crossed the room to my usual table, Allison matching me step for step, like an escort at a prison. Kylie looked up to scan the room for me and Mason, and I saw her look of confusion when she realized Allison was with me.

I said, "Kylie, meet Allison. She's new. Allison, this is Kylie."

Kylie's face lit up. She loved meeting people. "Hey, Allison, great to meet you."

I sat down opposite Kylie. Allison parked herself next to me just as Mason plunked his bag down across from us. "Hey, a new recruit," he said, smiling at Allison. "Glad to meet you. I'm Mason, by the way." He leaned over the table and held out his hand. Mason could be kind of a geek sometimes.

I watched Allison to see if she'd give him the rude act I'd been getting all morning, but something about Mason must have gotten to her. She shook his hand and even smiled a little when he pumped it up and down.

"This is Allison. She's new." I couldn't wait for tomorrow so she wouldn't be new anymore. "Mr. Smedley asked me to show her around."

"Are you serious?" Mason said, letting go of her hand and sitting down next to Kylie.

"Dead serious," I said. "Allison and I are part of a pilot program for new student integration." I raised my eyebrows to show what I thought of that.

"Get out," Kylie said, taking a sandwich and a packet of fruit snacks out of a brown paper bag.

"Nope, it's true," I said. "Right, Allison?" I looked over for confirmation, but she had turned back into the girl with the stone face. "Mr. Smedley said I was chosen because I'm respected by my peers."

"Well, that's certainly true. I respect the hell out of you," Mason said.

"Don't you have a lunch, Allison?" Kylie asked. Always thinking of other people, that was Kylie.

"I'm not hungry," Allison said.

"Neither am I," Kylie said. She put half her turkey sandwich on a napkin and pushed it across the table. "If you want it, it would save me from throwing it out." It looked pretty good. I could see a layer of lettuce and tomato, and I was betting there was some mayonnaise involved. If Allison didn't want it, I was tempted to take it myself.

Allison reached out and reluctantly pulled the napkin toward her. "Thank you."

"I brought a water, but I was thinking I'd rather have a soda," Mason said, pulling a bottle of Ice Mountain out of his bag. "Why don't you take this?"

"Oh no, that's okay," Allison said, but Mason was already up and heading for the lunch line. He had a kind of springy way of walking, all happy.

"So, Allison, where did you go to school before this?" Kylie asked.

"She's new," I said, to be funny, but Allison looked uncomfortable, not amused.

She bent her head to screw the cap off the bottle of water. "I just moved here. I used to live about two hours away. In a really small town." She reached around and played with the end of her braid. "My circumstances changed, so I'm here now."

Her circumstances changed? What was she, thirty years old? No high school student talked like that. I tried to catch Kylie's eye, to see if she was getting a weird feeling off Allison, but she didn't look my way. Instead she started telling Allison about Whitman. She pointed out tables in the lunchroom and gave her the rundown on who was okay and who to avoid. Kylie even threw in some trivia about one of the freshmen—turned out she was the daughter of one of the math teachers. *I* didn't even know that. By the time Mason came back with his Dr Pepper, Kylie was talking about the jock table. "They're okay," she said, "as long as you don't get in their way. Rae here made a huge mistake yesterday when she laughed at their leader, Blake Daly. He's the one in the Packer jersey."

"I couldn't help it. It was hysterical." I held up one of my carrot sticks. "First he was walking like this." I made the carrot bob up and down in an arrogant way. "And suddenly he's down on his ass, with his apple flying high and a slice of pizza on his leg." I made the carrot take a dive. "Mason caught the apple by whipping his arm out like this." I demonstrated. "I tried not to laugh, but the whole thing was too funny. I said I was sorry, but Blake's such a dickweed he didn't go for it. No sense of humor."

Allison listened politely while Mason joined Kylie in telling about the school—the football game coming up on Friday night, the assemblies that were lame except when the pompons squad performed, because they were pretty awesome. They asked about her classes, and Allison got her schedule out of her purse so they could look it over. Mason had three older brothers. All of them had gone to Whitman, so he knew all the teachers and could fill her in. I sat quietly eating my salami sandwich and carrot sticks, and watched. They hadn't given *me* this kind of info when I'd started out at the beginning of the school year.

By the time the bell rang, I was fully informed about Whitman High School. We all gathered up our things while Allison clutched her purse to her chest. When I went to stand up, I saw Blake Daly heading straight for me. He had a determined look on his face, and all I could think was that he was still pissed off from before. I couldn't believe he was going to make a big deal out of it. Yes, I laughed when he fell down, but I said I was sorry. I needed a comeback if he started up with me. *Get over it*—that's what I would say. Short and to the point. *Get over it*. He came up alongside our table, and I almost spoke the words before he even opened his mouth. Good thing I didn't because he wasn't coming to talk to me, he was there to talk to Allison. "Be in front of the school at two thirty." He spoke out of the corner of his mouth like he didn't want other people to see him talking to her.

She nodded.

"I mean it," he said. "Watch for my car. I'm not waiting if you're late." Then he disappeared into the crowd of students heading out the side doors.

I exchanged a look with Mason, who raised one eyebrow and mouthed *WTF?*

"You know Blake Daly?" Kylie asked.

Allison stood up. "He's my cousin."

Chapter 7

Flight Risk

The best thing about current events, my last class of the day, was that Kylie was in it too. She took over Allison duty, introducing her to the teacher and finding her an empty seat. I took my place on the opposite corner of the room and admired how smoothly Kylie handled the whole thing.

Kylie's a wonder. After you get over how short she is, the next thing you notice is her big smile and her amazing hair. She has this wonderful wavy golden hair, which actually glistens in the sunlight. It's soft like bunny fur. She says it's so soft because she uses a ton of conditioner to keep it from frizzing up, but I'm not sure I believe that. I've tried doing the same thing, and my hair just ends up looking flat and limp.

Allison sat in a desk behind Kylie's, and at one point I saw her reach out and touch Kylie's hair with one finger. When she saw me watching, she pulled her hand away, embarrassed.

She didn't look anything like Blake, so finding out that she was his cousin was a shock, especially since we'd just gotten through telling her the story about him falling down, and she hadn't said a word. And me with my big mouth, I'd called him a dickweed too. Or was it an asswipe? I couldn't remember. It wasn't nice talk, anyway. I hoped it wouldn't get back to him. That would be all I needed.

In the hall after lunch I asked her why she hadn't said her cousin went to Whitman, and she just shrugged. Blake didn't sound like he liked her much, but still, you'd think it would come up.

That day in current events, Mr. Goodwin had us making a collage of articles with a theme. We had a choice about the theme, as long as it was (surprise, surprise) a current event. Along with the collage we were supposed to write a three-paragraph paper describing the theme and how it fit into society today. It was the kind of busywork assignment I normally hated, but I liked using class time to cull through the pile of newspapers and magazines he had on the front table. As long as we looked busy, he didn't care what we did, so most of the kids were doing other homework, or sending text messages by holding their phones beneath their desks. Some of them were messaging each other, judging by the looks going back and forth. Allison looked through newspapers like she was actually participating, but I suspected she was just going through the motions.

Mr. Goodwin had a pretty good collection of news stuff—everything from the local paper to the *Wall Street Journal* and the *New York Times*. The magazines were mostly *Newsweek* and *Time* and those kinds of things, but I did run across an *AARP*, a magazine that, according to the cover, serves the needs and interests of people fifty and over. Mason or one of his brothers must have donated it to Mr. Goodwin's class, because the label was addressed to Edwin Mihashi. Figuring out that Mason's dad was at least fifty years old was surprising, because Gina was only thirty-five. Other people's parents were so old.

I came across an article about a man whose widow found out, at his funeral, that he had a whole other family three towns away. Then I came across another piece in *Newsweek* with research showing the importance of fathers to adolescent girls. I found another one about a woman who'd been adopted as a baby. She figured out, as an adult, that one of her bosses at a bank was actually her birth father. I wasn't sure where I could go with these articles, but I cut them all out anyway.

I was concentrating on deciding what kind of theme I had going here and was jotting down the words *"the breakdown of the family in modern society"* when Kylie came and tapped me on the shoulder. "Allison left," she said.

"What?" I looked up from my pile of cut-up newspapers.

"Allison just took off right this minute. I heard her make this funny noise like she was choking, and then she just got up and ran out of the room. I called after her, but she just kept going." She pointed to the door.

"She was *choking*?" Oh no, would they blame me if she died on my watch?

"No," Kylie said impatiently. "She made a weird noise in her throat, sort of like choking, but not really."

"Are you talking about that new girl?" The guy behind me, a wrestler named Ted, leaned in to join the conversation. "I saw when she jumped up. So weird. She ran out of the room like something was after her."

"Do you think I should go find her?" I looked from Ted to Kylie. "I'm supposed to be looking after her."

"Maybe you better," Kylie said. "It sounded like she was upset or sick or something."

I got permission to leave from Mr. Goodwin, who gave me a hall pass. He'd never heard of the new student integration pilot program, but I think he believed me. We only had half an hour left in the day anyhow, so it wasn't like I was missing out on much.

I put on my backpack and walked the hallways, unsure of how to do this. She wasn't anywhere in sight, and I wasn't about to start yelling her name. I looked in the closest bathroom, interrupting a couple making out by the sinks. The girl, who sat on the counter, was a sophomore like me. Her junior boyfriend stood in front of her with his arms wrapped around her waist. "What are you staring at?" the guy asked when I stopped just inside the door.

"Looking for someone," I said.

"No one here but us," he said. "Get lost." His girlfriend giggled, and they turned back to their fun.

I walked aimlessly, checking the health room and some other bathrooms until the bell rang. Now what? I stood indecisively while hordes of my fellow students poured out of classrooms on their way to freedom. Several minutes passed, and I was wondering what to do next when I suddenly remembered Blake Daly telling Allison he'd pick her up in front after school let out.

A few minutes later I was standing next to the glass doors that looked out onto the front parking lot. The buses picked up at the side entrance; the front was where the teachers and students parked. After school it was always crazy with kids driving through the parking lot, some of them honking and waving to get the attention of friends. I didn't see Allison among any of the kids lingering in front, and I also didn't see Blake's silver SUV. I might have missed them.

I breathed on the glass and ran my finger over the fog, making a peace sign. When I was a kid, I liked to think that the next person who tried this would see the sign and wonder if it meant something huge. Maybe it would result in some kind of worldwide phenomenon, like when people claim they've seen the

Virgin Mary and the place draws crowds. Now that I'm older, I know I don't have that kind of power.

I watched as kids walked past me, laughing and jostling each other. When I saw Nick Dunstan approach, I reached out and grabbed his sleeve. He surprised me by saying, "Hey, Rae." We'd had that weird exchange in the lunchroom during Blake's little problem with gravity, but I didn't realize he knew my name. "What's up?"

"Have you seen Blake? Mr. Smedley put me in charge of his cousin, Allison, and she took off. I don't know where she went."

Nick stepped in closer to get out of the way of the crowd. "No, I don't know where he is." He pulled a phone out of his pocket. "You want me to call him?"

"No, it's okay. She probably just left early and went home."

"Okay." He shrugged and gave my shoulder a squeeze. "If I see him, I'll tell him you were looking for him."

"Don't bother. I'll just tell Mr. Smedley she ditched me. I didn't want to be in charge of her anyway."

"I hear you." He shifted his backpack.

At the curb in front of the glass doors a red Mustang pulled up and honked three times in a row. In the driver's seat, Nick's girlfriend, Crystal, motioned impatiently with a broad sweep of her arm.

"That's my ride," he said. "Gotta go. Take care, Rae."

My feet dragged on the way to the office. How was I going to tell Mr. Smedley that I'd only been part of his pilot program for six hours and I'd already screwed up? What was Allison's problem?

I had to wait for Mr. Smedley, who, according to the office lady, was in a meeting but would be out shortly. I stood off to the side, idly looking through the items on the lost-and-found table. In grade school the lost items would be things like gloves and boots and lunchboxes. At the high school level you were more likely to find what I saw in front of me: a case for an iPod, gym clothes, a pair of Nike basketball shoes (size 11, I checked), and a letter jacket from someone who graduated last year, judging by the numbers on the sleeve. I wondered if the guy missed it.

Embarrassingly enough, I was going through the pockets of the letter jacket when the secretary told me Mr. Smedley was ready to see me.

"Rae," Mr. Smedley said as I walked into his office. He sat at his desk, his hand resting on a stack of file folders. "I've been thinking about you all day. How did Allison do?" He gestured for me to sit.

"Well..." How to phrase this? She was doing fine until she disappeared? I took a deep breath and parked myself in the chair opposite him. Out with it. "Actually, Mr. Smedley, that's why I'm here. I took her around and introduced her to all our teachers. She ate lunch at my table and was fine. At least she seemed fine. Although she was kind of quiet." I could hear myself talking faster. That always happened when I was nervous. "Maybe just because she's new? Anyway, it was going pretty well, I thought, until last hour, which is current events with Mr. Goodwin. We were working on an independent project and I didn't actually see her leave, but Kylie Johnson did. Kylie said she just got up and ran out of the room, like she was sick or upset or something. I've been looking for her ever since, but I haven't been able to find her."

Mr. Smedley's mouth formed a grim line while I explained. When I was done, he asked, "She didn't say anything before she left? Maybe to the teacher?"

I shook my head. "I'm really sorry."

"Don't worry about it, Rae. You did fine. I didn't expect you to be her bodyguard." He picked up a pen and tapped it on his desk. *Tap. Tap. Tap.* His forehead furrowed in what looked like disapproval.

I shifted in my seat. Could I leave now, or what? Finally I said, "I guess I wasn't the best choice for this program after all." I cleared my throat to ward off the lump that was threatening to get bigger. In a minute I'd be too upset to talk.

Mr. Smedley looked surprised. "Don't take this too hard, Rae. Things happen. I have the contact number for where Allison is living. I'll wait awhile and call to make sure she got home safely. I'll handle it from here."

"I really am sorry," I said, standing up.

He set the pen down and put his fingertips together to form a tent. "It's not your fault, Rae. Allison's just going through a tough time." He sighed. "Starting at a new school is never easy, even under the best circumstances." He took off his glasses and rubbed his eyes. When he looked up, he seemed different. Tired, older. Not the same man who bellowed in the halls and gave warning speeches at assemblies. "I would appreciate it if you'd continue watching out for her. Can you do that?"

"Okay," I said reluctantly. "Of course, I would have been nice to her anyway, but sure, I'll watch out for her."

"For some reason she's taken a special liking to you," he said. "I know it seems unfair to burden you with this, but if you'd stick with her for a while, I'd appreciate it."

I stood there, hesitating. I'd been hoping he'd let me off the hook, but no such luck. "I wouldn't say she's taken a liking to me," I said at last. "She barely talks to me. In fact, she's been kind of ignoring me all day. Maybe someone else would work out better for your new pilot program? I wouldn't mind if you found someone else to do it."

Mr. Smedley tapped his pen against the desk again. *Tap. Tap.* He looked up at me. "I have a confession to make, Rae. There isn't really a new student integration program."

"There isn't?"

He shook his head. "I just fabricated the whole thing so you'd agree to take Allison under your wing."

He lied about the pilot program? Could he do that? "Oh-kay," I said, not really understanding.

Tap, tap, tap, went his pen. "It was the only way she'd agree to attend classes. Her aunt and uncle enrolled her here, but she refused to come. Finally they talked her into coming in just for a tour of the school. Her aunt dropped her off for an hour yesterday, and I showed her around the school. She was very unimpressed, to say the least." He put his glasses back on. "I didn't think we'd be able to convince her to come here."

His pause was just a little bit too dramatic for me. "So what changed her mind?"

"You did, apparently."

I shifted in my seat. "I don't understand."

"When I showed her through the lunchroom, she saw you laughing. There was some kind of brouhaha with her cousin, Blake Daly?" He raised his eyebrows questioningly.

"He slipped on a wet spot near our table," I said, feeling my cheeks turn red. Mr. Smedley had seen the whole thing? "It just struck me as funny. He wasn't hurt," I added. "And I did say I was sorry for laughing."

"It's fine, Rae, it's fine. No one is upset with you. I just had to mention it because seeing you made Allison change her mind. When she first came in that day I'd mentioned pairing her up with another student, but she was having none of it. Then she saw you in the lunchroom and changed her mind. You were the only one she'd consider shadowing. It had to be you, or she wasn't coming to this school, she said."

"I don't get it. She just saw me laughing and picked me?"

"Yes."

How random. "You didn't tell her anything about me?"

"She asked who you were, and I told her your name. That's all I really knew about you." He held out his hands apologetically. "There are so many kids…"

"So, the whole respected by my peers thing, you just made that up?"

He looked a little sheepish. I had a feeling I'd struck a nerve. "I didn't make it up, of course not. I queried a few of your teachers, looked at your grade transcripts from your other schools. Everything checked out. I felt very confident in my choice." He pushed on the nosepiece on his glasses. "And I still have confidence in you. If Allison's in school tomorrow, act like nothing happened and stay with her just like you did today."

"Okay." I stood up, and Mr. Smedley rose up from his seat too. I was afraid he was going to walk me out, but instead he held out his hand. Awkward, but I could play along. I reached out and shook his hand, then released it and looked him straight in the eye. "I just have one more question before I go, Mr. Smedley."

"Yes, Rae?"

"When I apply to colleges, can I list the Rae Maddox Integration Program as one of my high school accomplishments?"

His face broke into a grin. "Of course. I'll even write a letter giving you complete credit for its creation and implementation."

"But we're not really going to call it that here at Whitman, are we?"

"Since it doesn't really exist, we won't be calling it anything."

"Good."

We said our good-byes, and he was all serious when he thanked me for coming in, but as I headed out of his office I thought I heard him chuckling.

Chapter 8

Gina, Interrupted

I took the long way home again, going past the kids' mental health building, this time using the sidewalk on the other side of the street. I wasn't taking any chances. As it turned out, my detour wasn't necessary since there was no sign of Paranoid Girl or any of the other kids. Staying after school to talk to Mr. Smedley had thrown off my schedule. I must have just missed them.

Speaking of mental health—and this is off topic, but somewhat related—here's something not too many people know: my mother was a patient in a psychiatric hospital when she was a teenager. Her story is that her parents had her committed after she'd stayed out all night, but my guess is there was more to it than that. My mom and her folks don't get along at all now, and it was even worse back then. "My stint in the loony bin," is what Gina called it, and I could still hear the bitterness in her voice. Gina was kind of a wild teenager, always up for new experiences—legal or not. This caused huge problems for my grandparents, Bob and Irene. In my mom's own words, she was the teenager from hell. In order to get her admitted to the psych hospital for a few days, her parents had to lie and say she was suicidal. Things went from bad

to worse after that, and she moved out of their house before she'd
even graduated from high school.

It's hard for me to imagine my grandparents the way my mom
describes them. We only visit once a year, but I think I have a
pretty good handle on who they are. Grandma Irene wears an
apron when she cooks, which is all the time. Her meals are wonderful, like Thanksgiving every day. She even makes waffles from
scratch. I didn't know that was even possible—I'd always thought
they came already made in the freezer section of the grocery
store. She's the kind of grandma who puts her hand on my forehead to check for fever when I'm not feeling well and sneaks into
the guest room in the middle of the night to cover me with an
extra blanket just in case I might be cold. Gina calls it smothering,
but I think it's wonderful.

Grandpa Bob has these corny jokes and does magic tricks
where he pulls five-dollar bills out of my ears and lets me keep
them. He does the crossword puzzle in the morning paper and
invites me along when he goes to the hardware store. During
one visit, I spent two days helping him install a new water heater.
Good times.

Their house is a tri-level with four bedrooms and three bathrooms. They were planning on having a bunch of kids I guess, but
all they got was Gina. And now me. Grandma's decorating style
is what Gina calls kitschy: braided rugs and lamps with wrought-
iron bases. The clock in the kitchen is a cat whose eyes move back
and forth. Grandpa calls him Felix. I think he used to be a cartoon
character or something.

It's so quiet at their house. Really quiet, like you can hear the
birds chirping on the back patio, and there's a ton of birds because of all the feeders. My grandparents' house always smells
good—no cigarette smoke, just cooking smells and the scent of

the Christmas tree, a real one, not like the junky one we set up on our end table in every apartment we've ever lived in.

When we visit for our week at Christmastime, Grandpa builds a fire in the fireplace and we roast marshmallows for s'mores while Gina goes out on the patio to smoke. She counts down the days until we can leave. The closer it gets to going home, the happier she is. I feel the exact opposite.

For the last four months we've been the closest we've ever lived to my grandparents—only a forty-five-minute drive away, but Mom still doesn't want to go see them. I talk to them all the time on the phone though. If she knew, she'd kill me.

I'm one of the few people who knows about Gina's stint as a mental patient. She told me how they strip-searched her when she first arrived and how they took everything away from her: her clothes, her lighter, her purse, and her watch. The watch had been a gift from her high school boyfriend, and she never got it back. The first night in lockdown she couldn't sleep at all because another girl was screaming and carrying on somewhere down the corridor. Like a wild animal, she said. "What kind of people would send their own daughter to a place like that?" she asked. I didn't answer. I almost said that there are two sides to every story, that maybe her parents acted out of desperation. Maybe. But I didn't say it, because I knew she wouldn't want to hear it.

One time, when Gina wasn't around, I asked my grandparents if they knew who my father was. Grandpa shook his head. "Sorry, Rae, she wouldn't tell us. We didn't see her for two years after she moved out, and then one Christmas Eve she just showed up with you in her arms. You were almost a year old by then."

"Best Christmas gift we ever got too," Grandma said. "I loved you from the second I saw your little face peering out of the hood of your snowsuit. You were such a beautiful baby. We were so happy to have you in our family." There were tears in her eyes, and she gave me a hug. I'm sure if they'd known the truth about my father, they would have told me.

So those are Gina's secrets, and here's one of my own: as badly as Gina wanted to escape Madison, that's how much I want to go back there. Grandpa took me once to the university campus in their town when I was about twelve. We walked around outside until our feet were cold and then went to the cafeteria for hot chocolate with whipped cream. The cashier gave me the once-over and said, "The freshmen look younger every year." Grandpa handed her the money, laughed, and said, "She's not a freshman yet, but just watch for her, she'll be here in a few years." When we got back to the car, he said, "You know, Rae, if you want to go to college here, Grandma and I will pay for it. You could stay with us or live in the dorms and use us as home base. We'd love to have you."

I nodded, but didn't say much. Gina would have been furious. She only visits over Christmas because they give her a thousand dollars in an envelope every year, and I get everything I ask for, practically. Buying our love, she calls it, but I think it's more of a bribe to make sure we come.

Right after that I formulated my plan. If I schedule my classes right, I'll have enough credits to graduate halfway through my senior year. My birthday is January 6, which is also the day I'll be getting on a bus to Madison and heading to the dorms. Hopefully we'll still live in Wisconsin because if we move back to Arizona or somewhere far away like that, it will be one long bus ride. Unless I fly, which I guess I could because I'll be a legal adult by then. I haven't worked out all the details yet, but I'm sure how it will end up.

My mother doesn't know about my plan. She thinks we're going to live together forever. In her mind, I'm going to graduate from high school, then take courses at some community college. She throws out suggestions for jobs I'd be good at—things like dental hygienist or pharmacy tech. They always need these, apparently, and they pay well. After I complete my course or get certification or whatever they call it, I will, according to her, go on to get a job in my new field. With two combined incomes in one household, Mom and I will be living the high life: vacationing in Vegas, renting a nicer apartment, maybe even setting a little money aside in savings. This is how she sees my future.

I've never told her that I have other ideas. I don't know *how* to tell her I have other ideas. She would be so angry with my grandparents, she'd probably never talk to them again, and it would be my fault.

If only there were two Raes—one to stay my mother's roommate, and another to go off to the university. That would make everyone happy. But I can't be two people, so I dread the future, even as I look forward to it.

I know when I leave it will break my mother's heart.

Chapter 9

Unlawful Entry

When I got to my apartment building, I noticed Gina's blue Saturn in the parking lot. Her work schedule changed from day to day, so I never knew what to expect. Even when she didn't have appointments, she sometimes stayed at the salon in case of walk-ins or to help the stylists out by taking a turn at the shampoo bowl. But she was here now, which was good, because I wanted to tell her about my day—how Mr. Smedley had admitted to making up a fictitious program in order to get me to help a new student, a girl with some kind of emotional problem. This was the type of story Gina would get into. She loved hearing about my day at school, all the better if I acted a scene out and did impressions. I could absolutely do Allison walking down the hall, not answering my questions, purposely ignoring me while sticking to my side every bit of the way. I looked forward to telling Gina about the couple making out in the bathroom and how Kylie told me that Allison just took off.

Opening the door to the apartment, I called out, "Hey, I'm home." I let the backpack slide off my shoulder, and it fell with a satisfying thud onto the shoe mat we keep in the entryway.

I heard laughter. "We're in here, Rae," Gina called out. Too bad she had company; my story would have to wait. I followed the sound to the kitchen. As I turned the corner and walked through the doorway, she said, "Here she is—better late than never. We've been waiting for you, Rae."

And I said…well, actually I didn't say anything at all because I was too stunned to speak. Completely at a loss for words. Struck dumb by the fact that in my own apartment, sitting in *my* chair at the kitchen table, was Allison. Yes, Allison. She sat across from my mother, fingers wrapped around a glass of Diet Coke. Her hair was no longer pulled tight into a French braid; instead, it hung in waves around her shoulders. Her patent leather grandma purse rested on the floor against my chair.

She sat there as relaxed as if she was the one who lived there, instead of me. I'd just learned the word "flabbergasted" in a vocabulary exercise in English. At the time, I doubted I'd ever get a chance to use it, but here I was—flabbergasted.

"Sit down, take a load off," Gina said, getting up to take a stack of magazines off our third kitchen chair. She turned to Allison. "See, I told you she'd be here soon. She always comes straight home. If not, she calls."

I sat down and cleared my throat, looking from my mother to Allison and back again. I said to Allison, "What are you doing here? I was looking for you."

"I missed my ride home," she said, avoiding the main issue, while stirring the crushed ice with her straw. "My aunt wasn't answering her phone, and I didn't know what else to do. It's too far to walk."

"You never mentioned having a friend named Allison," Gina said, giving my shoulder a poke and then getting up from the table. She set the magazines on the counter and opened the refrigerator, rummaging around for God knew what.

"I just met her today," I said to my mother's back. And to Allison I said, "How did you know where I lived?"

She shrugged. "I found you in the student directory last night, after I heard you were going to be showing me around. I wrote down your address and phone number for just in case. When I showed the crossing guard your address, she gave me directions."

"Good thing you had it with you." Gina handed me a bottle of water while looking at Allison. "Or you'd have been out of luck."

"So you live at Blake's house?" I asked.

Allison nodded. "For now." From the look on her face, I knew not to go any further with the questions. She'd put her wall back up. Just two minutes earlier she'd been laughing with Gina, but now she was the same unreachable girl who'd stuck to my side while looking down on me at the same time.

Gina, oblivious to the tension in the room, chatted on about the school and the neighborhood, ending up with, "Allison, you might not know this, but we just moved here not too long ago, didn't we, Rae?"

I nodded. "This is my first year at Whitman." I looked straight across the table at Allison. "So it's really odd that Mr. Smedley picked me, of all people, to be your guide. Why do you think he'd do that?"

And cool as could be, she shrugged and said, "Couldn't say."

"You should be honored, Rae," Gina said. "He must have thought you were the right person for the job."

"Oh, I got *that*." I pulled at the label on my bottle. "I just find it all very puzzling. I'd love to know the process, the reason I was chosen." I raised my gaze to see Allison staring back at me expressionlessly.

"Some things just can't be explained," she said, taking a sip through her straw.

"It just strikes me as being really odd," I said.

There was an awkward silence until my mother spoke. "Anyway," Gina said, "we've kept you long enough. If your aunt hasn't checked her messages by now, she might be worried. We better get you home."

Chapter 10

Lifestyles of the
Rich and Obnoxious

As it turned out, Blake Daly's house was bigger than my entire apartment building.

Allison, sitting in the front passenger seat, directed Gina through town, past the downtown business section, the industrial park, and outward to the newer subdivisions where all the rich kids lived. We pulled into the Dalys' circular drive, and the Saturn came to a rest, creaking as if it had old bones. The three of us sat in the car for a second, just taking it all in: the white columns, the concrete gargoyles standing guard on either side of the porch, the stained-glass double doors. Both doors depicted the same family crest, a shield thing that showed in pictures that Blake's ancestry could be traced to men who wore armor and jousted on horseback.

"Just the one family lives here?" Gina asked, lowering her sunglasses to get a good look.

"Just one," Allison said.

"Does Blake have brothers and sisters?" This from me in the backseat.

"Nope, he's an only child."

Gina whistled. "His dad must make some serious money to have a place like this."

Allison didn't answer; I heard the click of her seatbelt unfastening. "Well, thanks for the ride. I really appreciate it."

"No problem," Gina said. "Anytime."

Allison slung her purse over her shoulder and opened the door. "See you tomorrow, Rae."

Did I have a choice in the matter? No, I did not. Best to be nice. "Okay, see you then, Allison."

We watched her trudge from the car to the front door. She rang the bell and stood there for a minute or two. Blake finally came to the door with a scowl on his face and let her in. Allison turned to look at us one last time before she went inside.

Gina smiled and waved, and then she turned to me. "That poor girl. From the look on her face, you'd think she was heading into the lion's den."

"You got that right." Of course, if I had to stay in the same house as Blake Daly, I wouldn't be all sunshine and cotton candy either.

"Well." Gina tapped on the steering wheel. "Are you going to come sit up front, or am I going to have to act like a chauffeur on the way home?"

The chauffeur thing was tempting. We hadn't played that game in years, but I had a few questions for her and the conversation would be easier if I was up next to her.

As we headed down the driveway, Gina said, "Can you imagine shoveling all this? It would take forever."

"They probably pay someone to plow it."

"I guess you're right. That's how the other half lives. They have people to take care of all of life's little details."

I waited until we were on the main road before I asked, "So, Allison just showed up at the door, or what?"

"She knocked on the door, I answered it." Gina slowed for the turn. "To tell the honest-to-God truth, at first I thought she was selling something, the way she was dressed. She said she was looking for you. I said you weren't home yet, and she asked if she could wait. I said okay."

"You said okay and let her in? A complete stranger?" Honestly, sometimes Gina really lacked common sense.

Gina grinned. "She didn't look like a threat. I figured if she tried anything funny, I could totally take her down. I work out." She held her right arm toward me and flexed.

"I don't know about that. You might be stronger, but I wouldn't underestimate her. She has a lot of rage."

My mom frowned, but kept her eyes on the road. "Why do you say that?"

"She's just so hostile. Mr. Smedley said she specifically asked for me to be the one to show her around the school, and then when I did, she barely talked to me all day. And you heard how she denied knowing anything about me getting picked. I gave her a chance to say it was her idea, and she totally blanked out on me. I'm getting a definite anger vibe from her."

"I don't see it that way at all." The car bucked as she accelerated onto the main road. "When I look at Allison, I see a really sad, lonely girl. I actually wasn't too happy with you, Rae, back at home. Would it have killed you to be nice? You came off like you were accusing her."

Her words had a harsh tone that made me squirm. I wasn't used to my mother criticizing me. Usually she thought anything I did was "beyond reproach"—to use an expression we'd just covered in English. There was a silence between us for a long minute or two. Finally I said, "I didn't mean to act rude to her, but come on, she outright lied to me. That's not cool. Plus, I'm sorry but she just doesn't seem sad to me at all."

"Did you know that she's living with her aunt and uncle permanently now? She didn't tell me the circumstances, but it has to be something bad. She barely knows these people, but she needed a place to live and they were the only relatives who'd take her. She said they made it very clear to her they weren't real thrilled about it. The uncle works a million hours a week, and the aunt is totally into her career too. She's an accountant or something. And the cousin, the kid you know, is a little shit, she says."

"That's for sure."

"The only one who talks to her is the housekeeper. Imagine living *that* life."

The part about having a housekeeper didn't sound too bad. The rest of it would suck. "I didn't know all that," I said softly.

"Well, now you do."

Man, Gina was getting all worked up over this. She was starting to sound like other people's mothers. Was it my fault Allison wouldn't talk to me, but she'd confide in my mom?

"There's something about this girl, Rae. I can't even explain it, but I just feel like giving her a hug."

I looked out the window and watched as we passed the little shops that made up the city center. Outside the salon where Gina worked, one of her coworkers, Ben, was sweeping the sidewalk. Normally we'd slow down to honk and wave, but this time we just drove past.

"Would you do me a favor, Rae?"

"Sure."

"Could you be this girl's friend? She really, really needs one."

Oh, please, anything but that. "She doesn't *want* to be my friend, trust me. I'm telling you, Gina, I was nice to her all day, and she treated me like I was something nasty she stepped in."

"Could you just do it, Rae? As a personal favor to me? How often do I ask you to do something?"

Hmm, how often *did* she ask me to do something for her? Like, never? Hard to believe, but it was true—Gina didn't put any demands on me at all. Other kids talked about chores: taking out the garbage, cleaning their rooms, doing the dishes. Some even had chore charts or lists and they couldn't leave the house until everything was done, and done well. At my house there was none of that. Free and easy, that was our motto. Granted, I'd always done that kind of stuff without being asked. I mean, how hard was it to take a bag of trash out to the garbage can? Besides, I was born with a natural sense of order. Messes bother me. Still, I had to admit that my mom never asked for much, which made it impossible to say no when she did. "I'll be nice to her, of course I will. But being her friend—that I can't promise. If she doesn't want to be friends, there's not too much I can do about it. I mean, I can't hold a gun to her head and make her." That would make an interesting story: *How did you two get to be friends? Oh, she threatened to kill me...*

"Fair enough." Gina reached over and patted my arm. "By the way, I invited Allison to spend the night on Friday. I thought maybe you could invite Kylie and the three of you could listen to music or watch movies or something?"

I gave her my most exasperated look, and she laughed. "Come on, one night to help a little lost girl who needs a friend. Consider it an early birthday present to me."

An early birthday present? Ha! That was a reach. I'd rather have picked up something at the mall.

Chapter 11

Too Late Now

When we got home, my mom blended up two fruit smoothies, a popular meal at the Maddox house. Tonight's version was a particular favorite of mine—rice milk mixed with banana and fresh strawberries. She filled a large travel mug, popped the top on, and ceremoniously handed it to me. "Dinner is served."

"You shouldn't have gone to so much trouble," I said.

"Don't worry, I didn't."

I grabbed my backpack and went to my room to call Kylie and tell her the new development. She would die when she heard that Allison showed up at my house, won over my mother, and was going to be spending Friday night at my apartment. Of course, the Friday thing wasn't for sure yet. Allison still had to ask her aunt, but Gina seemed to think it was pretty definite. I was flabbergasted (that word again) when Gina announced she'd invited Allison without checking with me first, but I kept it cool. Once Gina set her mind to something, there was no point arguing. The deed was done. And I certainly wasn't going to be the one to *un*-invite Allison. How mean would that be? Plus, with Kylie there it would probably be okay. I'd never had Kylie to my house, but she was one of those sunshiny people you don't get sick of. If anyone could make the whole thing fun, it would be her.

I closed the bedroom door and fished my cell phone out of my backpack. We weren't supposed to take them to school, but everyone did. I kept mine on mute and sometimes forgot to turn it back on until later. Like today.

Sitting on the edge of my bed, I set the smoothie on my nightstand and flipped open the phone. Two messages. The first one was from Kylie: *"Rae, very important. Call me the instant you get this message. I have something huge to tell you. Huge."* The next message was also Kylie: *"Where the hell are you? I'm sorry but I had to tell Mason the news first. I was dying. It's about Allison. Call me."*

Kylie picked up on the first ring. Instead of the traditional greeting she said, "Where have you been?" Before I could answer she said, "You'll never guess what I found out about Allison."

My Allison news would have to wait. I eased myself back so that my head rested on my pillow. "Go ahead. I love gossip."

"It's not really gossip." Her voice softened. "It's actually pretty sad, and it explains a lot." She sighed. I could picture her twisting a strand of that soft hair around her finger. "After the bell rang, I went to clean up Allison's desk. You remember how we were looking at newspapers and magazines?"

"Yeah."

"I was just going to pick up the stuff on her desk and toss it on the pile up front. I'm not even sure why I looked at it, but I did. She was looking at the daily paper from a few weeks ago, and it was open to an article about her and her family. It was in that column that has news from around the state."

I sat up. "What did it say?"

"Oh it was so sad, Rae, so sad. It was just a small article, a few paragraphs, really, but it said that her whole house was destroyed by a fire. Her parents were sleeping in a bedroom upstairs and were killed. It said their only child, daughter Allison Daly, age sixteen, was the sole survivor."

"Oh my God." I thought about Gina's words: *Would it have killed you to be nice to her?* I felt terrible.

"I found another article about it online. It had photos. I sent you the link."

"Now I feel awful that I wasn't nicer to her."

"You *were* nice to her," Kylie said, defending me to me. "You showed her around, told her about the school, included her at lunchtime. You did all you could."

Her words relieved my guilt somewhat. "I guess." I looked up at the light fixture on the ceiling above my bed. It was a frosted glass bowl with a brass screw-on thingy in the center. Gina said it looked like a breast.

"Plus," Kylie continued, "you had no way of knowing what she'd been through. We can put more effort into making her feel welcome tomorrow."

Tomorrow. That reminded me of the sleepover looming later in the week. "Hey, Kylie," I said, "do you have any plans for Friday night?"

Chapter 12

Black and White and Read All Over

After I hung up with Kylie, I went straight to the computer, which sat on a beat-up desk Gina had acquired from a coworker who was moving. The same person also "gifted us" with a bread maker we'd yet to use and a clothing steamer we used all the time. Gina was a pro at getting something for nothing. Every time we moved, we left behind more than we took. Generally we only moved what we could fit in the car and a Hertz rental trailer. At each new city we started over, my mom scouring secondhand stores and curbside garbage piles for furniture. She was all about the challenge of putting together a new life, while I was the one yearning for what we'd left behind.

The computer was one of the things that always came with us. Gina didn't use it much at all. She craved human interaction—a metal box didn't do much for her. Even the TV couldn't hold her interest for long—before the first commercial she'd get up from the couch to make popcorn or check her voice mail. She was like those flies that spin around in circles on windowsills.

Kylie's e-mail was among others offering investment opportunities and penile enhancement. I deleted the spam before opening the one from Kylie and clicking on the link. It took me to the site of a small-town newspaper—the *Gazette*.

Even with Kylie's forewarning, the photos were a shock to me. Allison was featured in one of them—her freshman yearbook photo, from the look of it. The caption below it read, "Allison Daly, age 16, sole survivor of tragic fire." Next to her picture was another photo showing the firefighters trying to put out the fire. Even in the black-and-white photo the image was horrifying. Photographed at night, every window glowed against the dark of the sky. Fire haloed over the top of the roof and smoke surrounded the house like dark spirits in a horror movie.

A fire at 612 Magnolia Drive has claimed the lives of Steven and Tammy Daly, who were sleeping in an upstairs bedroom at the time. Their 16-year-old daughter, Allison Daly, the sole survivor of the fire, was found wandering disoriented in the adjacent woods. She was admitted to Memorial Hospital and treated for shock.

A neighbor, Jim Benson, driving home from a dart tournament, called 911 after spotting flames coming from the residence. Southfield firefighters were assisted by volunteers in fighting the fire, which broke out at approximately 3 a.m. Sunday, destroying the home, with an estimated $175,000 in damage. The cause is speculated to be a candle left burning on a wicker table on the front porch, according to Fire Marshall Fred Hanks.

At the height of the fire, firefighters were forced to exit as the roof started to collapse, Hanks said. "My men were heroic in their efforts, but we just got there too late. Every one of them was devastated that we weren't able to save Steve and Tammy," he said. "You couldn't find a nicer couple. This is a small community, and we're like family. It's just so tragic."

Funeral arrangements for the couple are undetermined at this time.

A link to a new page took me to a companion article headed by a photo of Allison's parents. They looked nice, really nice. He had his arm around her, and they both wore sunglasses and were laughing. A vacation photo, maybe? The article below the picture was a tribute to the Dalys. Their pastor said Steve was fond of telling how he met Tammy as a high school freshman. According to the pastor, Steve said that the minute he laid eyes on Tammy, he knew there was no other girl for him. I wondered how that felt, to know something like that instantly. Here I had trouble predicting which line would be fastest at the grocery store. The idea of picking a life partner by sight was beyond my comprehension.

The article said the couple was involved in their church: Tammy sang in the choir, and Steve was the treasurer. They took pride in their home and were always willing to lend a hand to neighbors, friends, and family. A few friends were quoted as saying that Steve loved to grill and have friends over, and Tammy used to be a Girl Scout leader. For Allison's troop, I wondered? The article didn't say.

In fact, Allison wasn't mentioned at all, except for one line at the bottom: "The couple is survived by their only child, daughter Allison Marie, a sophomore at Eisenhower High School."

I went back to the first article, the one describing the fire, and read it over and over again. Each time I felt a little sicker. I thought of Allison wandering dazed and confused, watching her house engulfed in flames from a neighboring field. Had she staggered out of the house thinking her parents had already escaped? I tried to imagine the acrid smell of smoke, the panic she must have felt.

I thought of how I'd feel if I lost Gina, and tears came to my eyes. Oh, I didn't want to feel this way. I wondered how Allison could stand it.

I wished I could rewind and do the day over again. I'd spent every minute of our day together wishing I could shake Allison off. I'd been mean, *so mean*, maybe not in the way I was acting, but in what I'd been thinking. I hoped it didn't show too much.

I thought too about what Gina said, how none of the relatives wanted Allison. That Blake's family took her in, but only reluctantly. How selfish was that? They had that big house and a housekeeper and everything and couldn't be bothered? And what was with Blake and his attitude? You'd think he'd be nice to his cousin, considering everything she'd been through.

I looked at the photo of Allison and searched her face. It wasn't a typical school picture. She wasn't even trying to smile, and her head was tilted down with her hair curtaining her face. Her expression was odd too, almost a little angry. No, not angry— more defiant, like she was determined not to cooperate with the photographer.

I stared at the photo and tried to remember where I'd seen that expression. Something about it was so familiar, like from a movie. No, not a movie. Where had I seen that look before? I concentrated. How frustrating not to be able to put my finger on it.

And then suddenly my mind put all the fragments together. Like kaleidoscope pieces they shifted in my memory, starting with the photo on my computer screen and going back to Allison sitting at the kitchen table with Gina. And before that, seeing

Allison in Mr. Smedley's office, bored and remote. And coming finally into focus, that same expression from a distance, staring at me from behind a chain-link fence at the Mental Health Unit for Children and Adolescents, urging me to keep moving.

Allison was Paranoid Girl.

Chapter 13

And Then Again, Maybe Not

When I got up the next morning, Gina was already sitting at the kitchen table, her hands around a mug. A plume of smoke rose from a cigarette on a nearby ashtray, and the scent of freshly brewed coffee filled the room. Why is it that coffee smells so good, yet tastes like crap? "Morning, sunshine," she said, turning to me with a smile.

"Kind of early for you, isn't it?" I asked. My mom was not a morning person. For years she'd staggered out of bed to see me off in the morning, but she never hid the fact that she found it painful. One day, in the middle of eighth grade, her birthday in fact, I released her from that obligation as a sort of gift from me. Truthfully, I liked having solitary time in the morning to eat, go online, and double-check my backpack. And she appreciated the extra sleep. I usually went into her room to say good-bye, but most of the time she didn't even remember me doing it.

Today was completely abnormal. Not only was she up, she was already dressed and ready for the day—her curly hair smoothed down and makeup perfectly done. She looked a little tired, but otherwise good.

"I didn't sleep very well," she said. "After you told me about Allison last night, I couldn't stop thinking about her. That poor girl! Her house burns down and her parents die and then she gets put in a mental institution?" Gina shook her head and tapped her cigarette against the side of the ashtray. I crossed the room to open the window a crack. The early morning October air had a bite to it, but it smelled fresh and crisp, like dew on leaves.

"It had to be horrible," I agreed. I got the milk out of the refrigerator and sat down to my place where a bowl, spoon, and my box of Lucky Charms sat waiting.

"I just keep imagining her in that terrible place. No one deserves that." She shook her head. "You have to find out how she wound up there. Did her aunt and uncle have her committed, or what? I'd love to know."

"I wasn't really planning on bringing it up," I said. "At least not right away. I don't really know her that well, and it's kind of personal, don't you think?" Truthfully, I wasn't sure how I'd bring up the subject, if I ever did. What would I say? By the way, I just happened to remember that you're the one I spotted at the mental health unit two weeks ago? Yeah, that would go over well.

Maybe if Allison hadn't been so indifferent to me yesterday it would be easier to connect with her. Despite the fact that she'd singled me out in the lunchroom, she didn't radiate goodwill in my direction. Things might get better with time, but I wasn't counting on it.

Gina took a drag from her cigarette. "I guess asking at school isn't such a good idea. Maybe when she's here for the sleepover?"

"Maybe," I said, pouring my cereal and then adding milk. "We'll see." I was starting to regret telling Gina my findings about Allison. She was taking it too much to heart.

"I have something for you to give her." Her forehead furrowed, and she reached down to the floor, lifting a filled plastic grocery bag the size of a throw pillow onto the table. It was sealed shut with clear tape.

"What is it?"

"Clothes." Seeing my questioning look, Gina said, "Allison told me that she didn't bring anything with her when she moved to her uncle's house. She's been wearing her aunt's things."

Well that would explain the middle-aged soccer mom look.

"Her aunt promised to take her shopping soon, when she's not," here she made finger quotes, "*so busy.*"

"Where did you get the clothes?"

"They're yours."

"Hey!"

"Don't worry," she said, grinning. "It's stuff you don't want. Those two pairs of jeans Grandma got you from the Gap, the ones that never fit right, and some tops that aren't black. I promise you, I didn't put anything in there you'd ever wear."

So that's how Allison went from standing out in the halls of Whitman High School to blending right in. I handed her the package first hour right after the bell rang. I had my doubts she'd even take it, frankly. I envisioned her rejecting it right off—saying she wasn't a pity case, or telling me that she actually liked dressing like she was forty-six. In my imaginings she threw the bag back in my face.

But she proved me wrong. I gave her the clothes, still sealed in plastic, and said, "My mom said to give you this." She looked suspicious, but opened it anyway. When she saw what was inside, she got a big smile on her face. It was the first time I'd seen anything resembling happiness. "They were mine, but I never wore them," I said.

"Okay," she said, nodding, and then she asked the teacher for a hall pass to go to the bathroom. Maybe part of her eagerness was due to what she was wearing: tan corduroy pants and a chocolate-colored turtleneck. The perfect ensemble for a luncheon with the Garden Club, but again, not so good for a high school sophomore.

When she came back, she had on my jeans, the ones I'd never quite liked. They fit her perfectly, none of the butt sagging I'd experienced. The shirt she'd chosen was a light blue V-necked tee, made to look like it had a lacy thingy underneath. Gina had gotten several of these cutesy tops from a coworker who'd cleaned out her closet and thought they'd be *perfect* for me. They were not. I knew as soon as Gina had brought them home there was no way I'd ever wear them, but on Allison the combination looked sort of good, and I got that sinking feeling you get when you give something away and then later wish you could take it back.

"Thanks, Rae, and tell your mom thanks too," Allison whispered. She crammed the package on the shelf under her seat next to her hideous patent leather purse. Today the purse held notebooks, folders, pens, and a calculator—the senior citizen version of a backpack. Maybe when her aunt's schedule eased up she could take her shopping for a new bag.

During the next two days, Allison opened up a little. At least she wasn't rude to me and listened when I talked. In class and at lunch she seemed to take part in things. Still, even though she was generally right next to me, I couldn't shake the feeling she wasn't quite there.

"Allison fits right in, don't you think?" Kylie asked on the phone one day after school.

"I guess."

"I give her a lot of credit, considering all she's been through."

"Yeah," I said. I had to give Allison that much—she'd lost her parents and her former life and yet gave no outward sign of any trauma. No public tears, no rage at the world. In the same situation, I'd be curled up like an embryo.

"I told her I admired how she was doing and said if she wanted to talk we'd be there for her."

"Wait a minute, you told her we knew about the fire?"

"I didn't say it like that—no, I just said I knew she'd been through a terrible time and that she was coping a lot better than I would. I said she could consider us friends she could talk to, if she needed someone to confide in."

"What did she say?"

"She just nodded and kind of gave me this sad smile. I think she appreciated that I brought it out in the open. I thought it was better that way. No secrets."

Thank God for Kylie. Clearly Allison needed all the support she could get, and Kylie was so good at that. Yes, she was just the right person to help a girl with emotional issues. They'd be friends long after I'd moved on.

Chapter 14

Tell Me a Secret

Our Friday night sleepover started with the arrival of Kylie carrying a Nike duffle bag almost as big as she was. Her dad came to the door with her and introduced himself to my mom, and then he gave Gina one of those real firm, serious handshakes. He was tall, more than six feet tall I'd guess, but he had the same sort of look as Kylie—big eyes and curly hair. Anyone could see at a glance they were father and daughter.

Kylie's dad gave her a big hug and kissed her forehead before he left. The kiss was extreme, he even made one of those "mwuh" noises, but Kylie wasn't the least bit embarrassed. She just laughed and hugged him back. It was kind of weird. Later I said, "Does he always do that loud kiss thing?"

She rolled her eyes and laughed. "God, yes. It's this thing he started at bedtime when I was little. He called it a magic kiss and told me it would keep bad dreams away. The funny thing is that I really think it works because I've never had nightmares." I must have had a funny look on my face because she added, "I'm sort of special to him. My mother calls it the only daughter syndrome. It really irritates my brothers—they say he favors me."

68

I always felt an empty twinge when girls said things like that. I wondered if I was some man's only daughter. And if that man even cared. If you were a guy who had a child out in the world, wouldn't you want to know how they're doing? Gina always bristled when I asked about my dad. She'd say things like, "I'll tell you about him when you're an adult," or "He's chosen not to be involved." I always felt like saying, *What about me? Don't I get a choice in the matter?* But I never said it. I could tell by the look on my mother's face when the conversation was over.

I'd overheard Gina tell other people things when she thought I couldn't hear. Different versions included an artificial insemination done on a dare (yeah, right), my father as a boyfriend who died in a car accident soon after I was conceived, and (my favorite), that my father was part of the Witness Protection Program and had to go into hiding.

I had my own theory, but it wasn't pretty. I almost hated to think it, but maybe Gina herself didn't know who my father was. She had a pretty wild past—lots of drinking and pot smoking. I'd heard of women being so drunk they didn't even remember what they'd done—that's another reason I don't drink, besides the fact that beer tastes terrible.

I always felt kind of left out when I saw someone with their father, especially if they get along like Kylie and her dad. I got ripped off in the dad lottery, face it. Kylie didn't even notice how quiet I got; she was too busy pulling DVDs out of her duffle. She was thinking *Underworld* would be a good movie to start with and then maybe *Darkness Falls*. Who knew Kylie had a dark side?

"What do you think," I said, "of saving these for another time? I think we should go with something funny, considering what Allison's gone through."

She twisted a strand of hair, thinking. "You have a point, but I was thinking that there's nothing like a scary movie to totally make you forget what's going on in your own life. They're kind of intense, but they're not depressing or sad or anything." She smiled widely to illustrate how *not* sad horror movies were. Fun, even.

"But look at this," I said, picking up *Darkness Falls*. "There's a *fire* right on the cover. Is it part of the story?"

Her cheeks reddened. "Oh God yes, I completely forgot about that." She grabbed the movie out of my hands and shoved it back into the bag. "Maybe that wouldn't be a good one after all."

By the time Allison arrived, we had it settled: *Underworld*, popcorn, Dr Pepper, and vitamin water. We also had *Mean Girls*, Doritos, Diet Coke, and Mountain Dew, as alternate selections.

Unlike Kylie, Allison was not escorted to my apartment by an adult—nobody walked in to meet us, no kiss on the forehead for her. She knocked on the door so softly that at first I just thought it was the refrigerator doing this thing where it clicks occasionally. By the time I opened the door, she was turning away as if she was giving up on a response. She held a white plastic garbage bag by its built-in drawstring loop and was wearing my jeans and another shirt I'd rejected—this one was cherry red with a snake sketched on the front. It looked cooler than I remembered. "Hi," she said.

I led her into the living room where Gina was talking to Kylie about nail health and cuticle care. Kylie was holding her fingers out and studying them.

"Hey, Allison," my mom said. "Welcome."

We'd agreed ahead of time that Gina would go out for the evening once my friends arrived. "Giving you some space," is how she put it. So she was going to be gone for most of the evening, but I had a sudden panicked thought that she could still ask Allison about the mental ward or the fire before she left.

Please, I thought, please don't ask any questions. Don't stay around and chat. I knew my mom wanted to help Allison, but it would be so awkward.

But I shouldn't have worried because Allison just said, "Thanks for the clothes."

And my mom said, "No problem." Then she gathered up her purse and cell phone and gave me the usual speech I get before she goes out for the night. That evening she and Carla were going to a comedy club to see someone they knew perform for open mic night. She didn't think she'd be out past midnight (she never thought she would be, but she usually was). Her cell would be on if I needed anything.

After she left, Allison said, "She trusts us to be alone?"

"Well, yeah," I said. "Why wouldn't she?"

I hadn't hosted many sleepovers in my life. Mostly I'd just been to other people's houses. Earlier in the day, I'd worried that the whole thing would be awkward, or that our tiny apartment wouldn't measure up. I knew there wasn't a *wrong* way to do it—it wasn't like the sleepover police would arrest me for contributing to the boredom of a minor, or anything like that. But still I wanted Allison and Kylie to have a good time.

I shouldn't have worried, though, because Kylie was a pro. Even before Allison arrived, she'd suggested moving the coffee table and propping the air mattress against the wall until we needed it. In front of the TV she created a nest out of comforters and pillows. She had a knack for this sleepover thing. I pictured her as a fourth grader starting up a game of Truth or Dare or dragging out the Ouija board.

"Movie first?" Kylie asked. "Or do you just want to hang out for a while?"

Allison shrugged and I didn't want to make the wrong decision, so Kylie took a stand. She put *Underworld* in the DVD player, told me to make popcorn, and put Allison on drink duty.

"You're a little bossy, Miss Johnson," I said.

She laughed. "I'm a little person, what can I say? If I don't speak up for myself, people don't give me any notice."

We turned out the lights and settled down in front of the glow of the TV, popcorn centrally located. The movie was pretty good—dark with lots of jumpy parts. It would have even held Gina's interest, I think, but Allison didn't seem to get into it. She was fidgety and distracted. About a third of the way through the movie I saw her check her cell phone. Halfway through she yawned loudly, like little kids do when they're acting in a school play.

We were clearly meant to hear it. Kylie, always considerate, paused the movie. "We can do something else if you want," she said, looking straight at her.

Allison acted all contrite. "If you don't mind. I don't want to be a problem, but it's just that I've seen the movie before." She'd already seen it? Before I could ask why she didn't tell us that before, she said, "I forgot I saw it. It was called something else when it first came out, wasn't it?"

Um, no. It was always called *Underworld*, but whatever.

Kylie quickly rose to the challenge. I was glad she was making it her problem. "I know what we can do," she said gleefully. "We can do that secrets game. We did it at my cousin's house, and it was so much fun."

That secrets game? Allison and I exchanged a glance that said neither of us knew what she was talking about.

"You really feel close to the other people when you're done, that's for sure," she continued. "It forces you to bare your soul."

"Is this the game where you do a shot when it's your turn?" Allison asked.

"No, no, no." Kylie laughed. "It's this therapy thing my cousin learned in rehab." She leaned in and lowered her voice. "That side of the family has big addiction problems. Really sad." She shook her head. "Anyway, what you do is, each person tells a secret, something they've never told anyone before. Something they wouldn't want other people to know. When you share like that, it forges connections—it tells the other people in the group you trust them not to tell."

"So you tell secrets. And this is a game how?" I asked.

"Okay, it's not really a game." Kylie sounded impatient. "But it's really cool, trust me."

Allison and I exchanged a skeptical look. I wasn't sure this was the best idea, especially for Allison, who, let's face it, wasn't your typical high school sophomore. She had to be emotionally fragile after everything she'd been through. Some things were better left unsaid. I didn't want her having a breakdown in my living room. Or anywhere else, for that matter.

"Come on, guys," Kylie said impatiently. "It can be anything. Even something from a long time ago."

"You go first," Allison said to Kylie, resting her elbows on her knees. "What's your secret?"

Kylie tapped a fingertip to her lips. "A secret, a secret, hmmm. I just had a good one. Wait, I'm not sure I can tell that one." She looked up in the air as if the answer would be somewhere above her head. "Did you want to go first, Rae?"

I shook my head. "It was your idea. I'll go next." I was a little short on secrets myself, but I could always make something up if

I had to. That was one of the few joys of always being the new girl. No one ever knew me well enough to contradict anything I said.

Kylie smiled brightly. "I've got it. This is my secret: my brother lets me drive when my parents are out of town."

"He does?" This was surprising—first that Kylie, who didn't even have a learner's permit, was out driving, and secondly that her brother would let her do it. Thirdly, why hadn't she ever mentioned it? We ate lunch together at school every day.

"Yep, he does. He tapes blocks of wood to the pedals so I can reach them and lets me drive him home from parties when he's been drinking."

So he didn't want to risk getting a DUI, but he'd let her risk getting caught driving without a license? That was so messed up. I almost said as much, but just then Allison interrupted. "Cool," she said. "Do you get to go to the parties?"

"Yep. Twice we've done it, and I've hung out with his college friends."

"But didn't you feel kind of weird being at a college party?" I asked.

She shrugged. "I did at first, but Andy's friends totally love me. They say I'm their mascot. They like to pick me up and carry me around."

"And you like this?" I glanced over at Allison, who looked enthralled to hear this new insight into Kylie's life.

"Oh yeah, it's really funny. One time one of the guys put me on top of the refrigerator. For decoration, he said. I sat up there for like an hour. People would open the fridge door to get a beer, and some of them were so drunk they didn't even notice me. I'd say something and it would scare the hell out of them."

"What would your parents do if they found out?" Allison asked.

"Oh my God, they'd kill us. I'd probably never be able to get my driver's license. And God, it would really be bad for Andy. They'd probably kick him out, and he'd have to live on campus, and he can't really afford that. Basically it would ruin our lives." She said it pretty cheerfully, considering. "Andy would be furious if he found out I told you. I promised not to tell *anyone*."

"Great secret." Allison nodded approvingly.

Kylie turned to me, cheered at having gone first. "Okay, Rae, your turn. Time to confess your deepest, darkest secret." A minute ago any secret would do, but now it had to be my deepest, darkest secret? I was so screwed. "See if you can top mine."

A challenge. I really wasn't comfortable with this. I'd planned on saying something about my father—the whole *I don't know anything about him* story. How Gina's explanations never gelled, how my grandparents didn't even know of my existence until Gina showed up on my doorstop when I was a toddler. But it wasn't really much of a secret. In fact, Kylie had already heard most of it.

"Unless you don't have anything?" Allison said.

"No, I have something." And then—I'm not sure why I blurted this out, it wasn't even in my mind to tell—I told them the thing I wasn't ever going to tell anyone. The one secret I had that could devastate someone. "This is my secret: I'm leaving my mother."

"You mean like running away?" Kylie asked.

"No, I mean when I turn eighteen, I'm going to graduate early and go to college near my grandparents' house in Madison."

They both looked disappointed.

"That's it?" Allison said.

Kylie's forehead furrowed. "Maybe I didn't explain this right. It's supposed to be a real secret. Something you don't want found out." She placed a sympathetic hand on my shoulder. "Almost everyone is planning on graduating and going to college. That doesn't really qualify as a secret."

"No," I protested. "It's more than that. My mom has no idea I have this planned. She thinks I'm going to graduate in June and go to some local college and still live with her. And she can't stand my grandparents. If she knew they'd offered to pay for my college and to live with them, it would kill her. She's going to feel like I stabbed her in the back. It's going to be like I went over to their side, like I turned my back on her."

They still didn't look convinced. "Maybe," Allison said, "this isn't the big deal you think it is. For all you know, your mom will be glad to see you go. Maybe she's been waiting for you to grow up and move out so she can really start living."

Kylie nodded in agreement. "My folks say stuff like that all the time." She cocked her head to one side and lowered her voice. "'Once the kids are out, we're going to travel. After Kevin graduates, we're going to remodel the bathroom. When it's just the two of us left, we're replacing the carpeting.' Like having us around is holding them back."

"My parents used to say that as soon as I was off to college they were going on a two-week trip to Hawaii." Allison looked down at the floor as she spoke, her voice raw with emotion. "They were going to go for their twenty-fifth wedding anniversary." She clutched her can of Dr Pepper so tightly the metal crinkled.

The room was quiet for a moment, and then Kylie went over to give her a hug. "Oh Allison, I'm so sorry." She patted Allison's back softly and mouthed the words *say something* in my direction.

"I'm really sorry too," I said, echoing Kylie. What else could I say? When Allison started crying, big tears that dripped onto Kylie's shoulder, I said, "I'll get some Kleenex," and darted off to the bathroom. I wished I could be more like Kylie. She slid into the friend-comforter role like it was nothing. I felt for Allison, I really did, but something held me back from saying all the right things, from giving her a hug. It was a line I was afraid to cross.

When I got back, I handed Allison the Kleenex box, and she pulled one out to dab at her eyes. Kylie patted her back and said, "It'll be okay," over and over again. This seemed to go on for a really long time. It occurred to me that this had to be the worst sleepover ever.

"What would make you feel better?" I asked. "We could put on a CD." I jabbed a thumb at Gina's old stereo, more of a big boom box kind of thing, really, but it was all we had. "And we could make brownies or Rice Krispie Treats." Food always cheered me up.

Allison sat up straight, disengaging from Kylie's arms. "There is something we can do that would make me feel better." She blew her nose loudly.

"What is it?" Kylie asked.

Allison finished with her nose and then pulled another Kleenex out of the box to wipe her eyes again. By now they were red and puffy. "I just want to get out of here for a while. No offense, Rae." She nodded in my direction. "But I just feel like if I get some fresh air it will take my mind off things."

"We could walk down to the 7-Eleven," Kylie suggested. "I know one of the guys who works there, and he gives me my Slurpees for free."

Free Slurpees, that was a pretty sweet deal. We looked to Allison for her take on it.

"No." She shook her head. "Nothing personal, Kylie, but I have a different idea. You guys want to go to a party?"

Chapter 15

Party Crashers

From there things just spiraled out of control. Not my fault, really. I mean, I wasn't the one who invited Allison in the first place, and then it was just supposed to be a girls' night with movies and gossiping and junk food, but the next thing I know we're driving across town, with Kylie's brother Andy at the wheel.

The party Allison wanted to go to was a bonfire at her own house. Well, Blake's house, really. Blake didn't want her there—to keep Allison away, his mother had planned to take her shopping in Chicago and stay the night, something Allison absolutely did not want to do. As it turned out, my invitation saved her from the forced bonding with her aunt. I could tell that it really burned her, no pun intended, that Blake hadn't included her in this bonfire get-together with his friends.

And what was with Kylie? In about two minutes' time she was totally into the idea, helping plan how we could get there (her brother) and saying we could spy on Blake and company. Somewhere in there I tried to be the voice of reason, saying that those kids weren't worth bothering with—did we really need to be acting like seventh graders by hiding in the bushes spying on them?

I was ignored and then swept along into the insanity. In the car I felt a teeny bit better because I got to ride shotgun. Kylie's brother was really cute, and I liked his music. He also drove kind of fast. When he cornered it, Kylie and Allison did the leaning to one side that's always amusing if you're in the right mood.

"You'll pick us up too?" Kylie asked Andy, in between songs.

"I said I would, didn't I?" Andy said. He smiled at me like, *Kids, they never listen.* "I'll have my cell on. Just call."

I grinned back at him, glad to be in on it.

Allison had Andy drop us off a few houses down from Blake's. So we could sneak up on them, was the way she put it. She and Kylie were laughing now. "Thanks for the ride," I said to Andy.

He shrugged. "No problem. I'm not doing anything until later anyway."

We got out of the car, and Allison led the way toward Blake's house. There were cars lined up and down the street, the kind of cars rich people give their kids so they can be the cool parents. There were Jeeps and Mustangs, a Lexus, and a Mini Cooper, and those were just the ones I recognized.

"This way," Allison hissed, cutting through several neighbors' yards. I hoped there wouldn't be any large dogs or security systems, but Allison knew her stuff and it was a safe route. At one point we walked around a large pool illuminated by dim lights at ground level. On the far end a fake waterfall ran continuously. The air was chilly, but I could tell from the vapors that rose off it that the water was heated. I imagined hot days by the pool, a cold drink in hand. Answering my cell phone and telling my friends, "Come on over. I'm just hanging out by the pool." In my daydreams I had tons of friends. Off in the distance I could hear Blake's party in progress, the whoops and hollering that accompanied underage drinking.

"Come on, Rae," Allison urged.

Kylie backtracked and playfully grabbed my arm. "Rae, hurry up."

We circled around the back of Blake's lot and stopped in a spot where we were conveniently shielded by a row of pine trees. About twenty feet in front of us, a fire burned brightly. I'd been expecting one of those outdoor fireplaces, but this bonfire was built right on the ground with large rocks surrounding it. Logs were teepee-stacked in the middle. Clustered all around the fire were Whitman High's most popular sophomores and juniors (at least in their opinion), some sitting in canvas stadium chairs, but most standing. The smell of a campfire was something I'd always adored. As much as I hadn't wanted to come, I had to admit that this whole thing—the secretiveness, the chilly air, the smoke scent—was pretty exhilarating.

Next to me Kylie shivered with excitement. "This evening just got a lot more interesting, hey?" she whispered, nudging me.

I nodded in agreement. The kids in front of us were a bunch of self-absorbed egomaniacs showing off for each other, but from this vantage point it was fascinating in a reality show kind of way. Blake had his arm around a blond girl. I couldn't place her, but she looked like that type you see around school, the kind with pouty lips and shiny, sleek hair. The kind who wore flip-flops and shorts all year round.

There were about twenty kids total. Most of the party goers held cans of beer. Some had soda. It was easy to spot the ones who were drunk—they laughed doubled over, the girls hung on their boyfriends, everything about them was loud and exaggerated.

A few of the kids seemed to be flying solo. The single guys were in pyro-mode, dropping plastic bottles into the flames. The unattached girls lingered nearby and encouraged them with laughter and shrieking. It was all very tribal.

Once my eyes adjusted, I could see more clearly. Kylie and Allison moved a little closer, scooting up to another group of bushes on the left, but I had a good view from where I was, so I stayed put. If I concentrated, I could hear every word. One of the football players, a kid they called Jocko, pulled up his shirt to show off his stomach, which he was able to puff out so he looked eight months pregnant. When one of the girls said, "How did you do that?" he patted his belly and looked very pleased with himself.

This started a competition of stupid human tricks—one girl was double jointed and could pull her thumb all the way back, and her boyfriend could roll his eyes upwards until only the whites showed. Another guy took off his shirt and made his pecs dance. You get the picture. None of them impressed me until Nick Dunstan got up to juggle cans of Mountain Dew. He started with two, and once he got going one of the girls tossed him a third. With the fire behind him it was an awesome sight. When the girl threw yet another one, he said, "Whoa," and stepped back. I thought he was going to drop them, but he recovered and added the fourth to the loop.

He had their attention now, and the other kids moved so they were gathered around him. Before it got anti-climactic, Nick spun around while still juggling, then ended it by saying, "Think fast," and tossing each can to a specific person in the crowd. When he was done, he bowed dramatically. A few of the girls clapped.

"Thank you, thank you. I'll be here all week. I do accept tips," he said.

"Oh, Nick," a girl, sloppy drunk, said, "you're so good with your hands."

"That's not what Crystal said," Blake bellowed, and then he made this fake laughing noise—*haw, haw*—*only kidding*.

Nick turned away, and for a split second the flames illuminated the hurt look on his face.

"Blake, that was so mean." This from Blake's blond sidekick. She used a stage whisper, not realizing apparently that everyone could hear her. "He can't help it if Crystal dumped him."

So that was it. Come to think of it, I hadn't noticed Crystal in the gathering, and she was sort of a leader in that pack. Kylie had said Nick was only included in that group because he was one half of the Nick/Crystal couple. Why was he there when she wasn't?

Blake wasn't letting it drop. "So *where* is Crystal tonight, Nicky?"

Nick turned to face him. "She had other plans."

"Yeah, I bet she did. Other plans with someone else, is what I heard. You're so finished, my friend."

A flicker of anger crossed Nick's face, but he held back. When he did speak it was through clenched teeth. "So Blake, here's a question for *you*. Why isn't your cousin Allison here tonight?" It got quiet suddenly. Nick definitely had the floor. "Don't you think it would have been nice to let her meet all your friends? Since she's new and all?"

In the shrubbery where Allison and Kylie hid, I heard a rustle. I held my breath waiting for his answer.

Blake only paused for a moment, and then he made that annoying *haw, haw* noise again. "Trust me, you don't want to hang out with that psycho bitch. She's so stupid she burned down her own house and killed her parents. And now I'm stuck with her."

Chapter 16
Allison Crashing

Allison wailed loudly, an inhuman sound that pierced the night air and made me stiffen in alarm. Everyone turned to look for the source of the noise, and at the same second she tore out of her hiding place and threw herself at Blake. The blond girl who had an arm around his backside stepped away, shocked.

"Bastard," Allison yelled, hitting Blake's chest with her fists. "How can you say that, you bastard?" She screamed and hit at him over and over again as if possessed.

"Hey," Blake said, trying unsuccessfully to hold her off him, while the rest of the group looked on dumbstruck.

"Lying bastard. You lie, you lie, you lie." Blake had the size advantage, but Allison had a lot of anger.

"Stop it!" Blake grabbed hold of her wrists, and she responded by kicking at him. "See what I mean?" He addressed his friends over the top of her head. "She's a mental case."

"Why do you have to be so mean?" Allison yelled. "They're dead, my parents are dead. I have nothing left."

Kylie came out into the circle and stood behind Allison, who was now sobbing. "Leave her alone," she said. "Let her go." Little

Kylie braving hostile territory and facing the giant. So much courage in one tiny little person. I knew I should join her, but I was frozen to the spot by my own cowardice.

"Hey, Kylie," one of the girls said in a friendly way. Everyone knew Kylie. She was well liked around school.

Kylie nodded at the girl, but didn't move. She patted Allison's back. "It's okay, Allison. Nobody listens to Blake anyway. Let's just go. It'll be okay. No one believes him." Even over Allison's sobs, her words were clear.

The girl who could pull her thumb all the way back stepped forward. "Don't cry, Allison. It's okay." As I looked at the faces of the kids watching this spectacle, it seemed they were sympathizing with Allison. It did look bad—this hulking football player physically restraining a much smaller girl by her wrist, sneering while she cried.

"Let's just go, Allison," Kylie repeated, glancing in my direction. I almost stepped out then, but something held me back. Maybe it's because I'd then become the center of attention, something I always hated, and in the process wind up casting my lot with Allison. Did I want that?

Blake released his grip and pushed her away roughly. "Yeah, just go. No one wants you here, anyway."

Allison stumbled backward and wiped her face with the back of her hand.

"Come on, Allison." Kylie reached out to take her arm, but Allison shook her head and took off running on the far side of the bonfire. Kylie followed her into the dark of the night, and there I stood, left behind. Off in the distance I heard Kylie's voice. "Wait, Allison!"

From Blake's house came the sound of a door opening and a woman's voice. "Blake, is everything okay out there?"

"Yes, Mom, everything's fine." Exasperated.

"Do you kids need any more snacks or soda?"

"I said we're fine."

The door shut and Blake's group started talking quietly amongst themselves. "You weren't very nice to your cousin, Blake," a girl said, accusingly.

"*She's* the one who's not nice," he answered.

Good comeback, Dr. Phil.

So now I was screwed. I couldn't follow Kylie and Allison without giving myself away, unless I circled way around the party. Unless, and here was a thought, they'd gone back to the spot where Andy had dropped us off. That would make sense. I could backtrack the way we came and meet up with them there.

I retreated quietly through the bushes and past the neighbor's pool—still lit up, the waterfall running. Man, I'd hate to see their electric bill.

When I reached the road, I started breathing a little easier. Certainly Kylie would think to find me there. It made sense.

Reaching into my pocket for my phone, I felt a pang when I realized I'd left it at home. How stupid was that? Most of the time it was glued to me, but when I needed it most I didn't have it. I could picture right where I'd left it too—right on my computer desk next to the mouse.

I walked to the exact spot where we'd exited the car, looking up and down the street as I went. The houses all had matching lamp-posts next to the driveways and most of them had lights on inside as well, but there weren't any streetlights like in my neighborhood.

The night air, which had seemed so invigorating before, was now cold and clammy. All I wanted was to meet up with my friends and go home. This evening was turning out to be a disaster.

I waited for what seemed like forever, but it probably was only half an hour. With no watch and no phone I had no way to tell the time. A car drove past at one point, but it was no one I knew, just an old couple who eyed me suspiciously as they passed.

Screw it, I thought finally and started walking toward Blake's house. If I didn't encounter Allison and Kylie along the way, I could go up to the house and ask Mrs. Daly if I could use their phone. She wouldn't know if I was in his group of friends or not. Generally parents loved me. Such a nice girl, so polite and friendly.

Chapter 17

Just in the Nick of Time

Mentally I practiced my plea to Blake's mom as I made my way toward the house. *Hi, I'm one of Blake's friends. I was down at the bonfire when I noticed my cell phone battery is dead. If it isn't too much trouble, could I use your phone to call my mom?* No, TMI. Maybe, *Blake said it was okay to use your phone. I need to call my mom for a ride.* But wouldn't I need to explain about my phone? This whole thing made my head hurt.

As long as Blake wasn't around, anything I said would be okay, I decided. Then I'd call Kylie and we'd work out how Andy could pick me up. My only other options were calling my mother or walking for miles. Neither one appealed.

I concentrated on one foot in front of the other. I really didn't want to knock on the door and talk to Blake's parents, but I was out of ideas. I could hear the party again, the muffled sound of rap music (yuck) and loud talking along with some obnoxious laughter.

As I walked along the row of parked cars belonging to my wealthier classmates, I had a heart attack. Or nearly had one, any-way. I was still working on my speech to Mrs. Daly (what sounded better—*My cell is dead?* or *My phone's not working?*) when something grabbed my sleeve. "Oh my God," I yelled. Looking down I saw a hand attached to an arm belonging to Nick Dunstan. He was sitting in a pickup truck with the window down and the engine off. If he hadn't grabbed my sleeve, I would have walked right past him. "Don't *do* that," I said, swatting at him. "You scared me."

"I'm sorry." He did look sorry. "I said your name, but you were in some kind of trance or something. Your lips were moving."

"Oh."

"What are you doing here?"

"Me? I'm looking for my friend Kylie." Basically the truth.

Nick sighed. "She was here before, with Blake's cousin Allison, but they left." He tapped his fingertips on the steering wheel. "Hey, can I ask you for a favor? Would you give me a ride home?"

Talk about confused. First off, did he not see me walking? Secondly, I didn't even have my license yet. "I don't have a car," I said. "I got dropped off."

"Oh," he said glumly. "Too bad. I really need to get out of here."

"Is there a problem with your truck?"

"I'm parked in." He jabbed a thumb front and back.

I took a step back to assess the situation. Sure enough, he was locked in. My guess was that he didn't want to go back to the party and ask the owners to move their cars. Understandable, considering what had happened. "I think if you maneuver back and forth a few times, and back up onto the grass, you can get it out. I can talk you through it, if you want."

"Would you?" He grinned. "That would be great."

I called out directions, and he inched the truck back and forth, angling it a little more each time, until there was enough space to ease it forward. In order to get out of his space, he had to drive partway onto Blake's neighbor's lawn, but I don't think he left tire marks. Not any I could see, anyway.

"Thanks, Rae," he said, once he was free. "I'm not sure what I'd have done if you hadn't come along. You're a lifesaver."

"I'm glad I could help." I leaned in to talk. "Do you think *you* could give *me* a ride home?"

Unlike my mom's car, the inside of Nick's truck was really clean. No fast-food wrappers or bank slips. No Starbucks cups. It smelled clean too, because of the pine tree air freshener that hung from his rearview mirror. I gave him directions to my house. He knew exactly which apartment complex I meant.

"So," I said, as he turned out of the subdivision, "did Crystal come in a different car?"

If I was looking for a reaction, I didn't get it. His face didn't give anything away, and his voice was steady. "Nope," he said, almost cheerfully. "Crystal wasn't here tonight. She's now going out with Trey Griffin."

"Oh, I'm sorry." Secretly I'd always wondered how Nick and Crystal ever got together in the first place. Crystal was so flaky that Mason referred to her as "Crystal Light," while Nick seemed to have it all together—smart, funny, personable.

"Yeah, I'm sorry too. It happens, I guess. You think a person's a certain way, and they turn out to be different." He turned on the radio and scanned a few stations, then shut it off. "How about you?"

"What about me?"

"Are you going out with anyone?"

"No." Oh damn, I said it too quickly, like of course I wasn't going out with anyone, who would go out with me? "I mean, not right now."

"Good to know." He smiled in my direction for just an instant. It was a shy smile, but unmistakable in meaning.

My heart quivered a little. Nick Dunstan was flirting with me, I was sure of it. This was momentous. I didn't have a lot of experience in this area, but I knew I should say something back. If only I could think of the right thing—

"So, Mr. Smedley put you in charge of Allison," he said, before I could come back with my own really smooth flirtatious comment. "How's that working out?"

Relieved at the change of subject, I told him everything, starting with how Mr. Smedley tricked me into being Allison's guide, to how Kylie found the newspaper article online, and how my mother took pity on Allison and invited her to sleep over. Even how Kylie and Allison decided to spy on the bonfire party. I left out the part about me also being in the bushes though, and made it sound like I'd only arrived later.

Somewhere in there I remembered that Kylie and Allison were still out in the world wondering where I was. Instead of asking Nick for a ride I should have asked to use his cell phone, but it honestly hadn't occurred to me. Now here I was, driving away from the place where I'd last seen my friends. I should have felt guilty. Instead, I wanted this ride to go on forever.

We got to my place way too quickly. "This is it," I said, pointing to the building. "The one with the lights on." Compared to Blake's neighborhood mine looked a little seedy, actually. Thank God, Nick pulled up in front. If he'd dropped me off in the back, he'd have seen the graffitied dumpsters and the junker car our upstairs neighbor had up on blocks. Said neighbor was going to fix it—that was the story, anyway—but I didn't see it happening. "Thanks for the ride, Nick. I really appreciate it."

As I unfastened my seatbelt and went to open the door, he reached over and touched my arm. "Rae?"

"Yes?"

"So you live here with just your mom?"

Where was he going with this? "Yep, just the two of us." I was always afraid that people would think my mom and I were the stereotypical white trash family—the manicurist unwed mother living with her teenage daughter in an apartment on the wrong side of the tracks. I was ready for a smartass comment, or questions about my fatherless state. If Nick was going to judge me, I was ready with a comeback.

"Do you think your mom would mind if you and I went out sometime?"

Okay, I was wrong. Oh, I was so glad to be wrong. "No, I don't think she'd mind at all."

Nick ran his fingertips up my arm and then brushed lightly along my jawline, giving me a shiver of pleasure. "Good. I'd like that." He drew back and sat upright. "I mean, if that's okay with you."

"That's okay with me."

His eyes locked on mine, and he leaned toward me again. Instinctively I leaned in too, knowing he was going to kiss me, *wanting* him to kiss me. His lips brushed mine, and I caught the faint scent of beer on his breath. Our lips had just met when he pulled back. "Is that your mother at the window?"

"Where?" I whipped around to see a silhouetted figure framed by my living room window. I couldn't see the face, but the person was short with curly hair. Kylie. Apparently they made it back before me, and Kylie remembered the secret key Mom and I kept on top of the doorframe. "No, that looks like Kylie. She and Allison are staying over."

"Yeah, you told me. It was your mother's idea."

I waited a second to see if we could get the moment back. I was willing to settle for a good-bye hug or a kiss on the cheek—*anything*. Apparently, though, the doorway of opportunity had slammed shut.

"I'll see you at school then, okay?" he said.

It was a dismissal if ever I heard one. What happened next is so out of character for me, I can barely believe I did it. As I was about to close the car door I paused and said, "Why don't you plan on eating lunch at my table on Monday?"

"Maybe. Sure, I could do that." He looked thoughtful. "No, wait, count on it. I'll be there for sure."

Chapter 18

Kylie in Waiting

Kylie met me at the door in worried-mother mode. "Rae, thank God you're here! I wasn't sure what to do, if I should call your mother, or go look for you—"

"You didn't call my mom, did you?"

"No, but I was going to." She led me into the living room, to show me Allison sleeping on the air mattress. From the light of the hallway, I could clearly see her sprawled on her back, one arm lifted over her head like she was about to wave. Her chest rose and fell with each breath. "I have so much to tell you." Kylie was whispering now. "I feel terrible that we left without you, but Allison was hysterical, and she ran through all these people's yards. We wound up like three blocks away, and Andy came right away when I called. You weren't answering your phone, so I didn't know what to do. Don't be mad."

"I'm not mad."

She motioned for us to go into the kitchen. I got two sodas out of the fridge, and we sat at the table. The only light in the room came from the bulb over the stove. "So who drove you home?"

"Nick Dunstan."

"Oh, he's so nice. You missed it, but there was a big showdown with him and Blake at the bonfire. Nick asked why Blake didn't invite his cousin, and Blake said Allison was a psycho bitch." Kylie's face contorted in anger. "Blake is such an asshole—he said she burned down her house and killed her parents, and he said it loud enough for everyone to hear. We were standing right there in the bushes when he said it. It was so terrible, Rae. If you had heard the horrible noise she made when he said it." She shook her head. "She was in so much pain. Then Allison ran out and started hitting Blake and screamed that he was lying, and he started making fun of her. Then we left, like I told you. I didn't know where you went and Allison was having a breakdown, so I kind of concentrated on helping her and hoped you would call or something. You aren't upset with me, are you?"

"No, it was just a big mix-up. I'm glad you handled things."

"I kept thinking you'd come out when Blake was being so mean to Allison, but you never did. Where were you?"

"Me?" Think fast. "I went back to look for my cell phone. I must have dropped it when we were going through all those yards. I never did find it. And when I returned to the bonfire, you guys were gone." Good lord, I was a quick liar. I pulled that one right out of my butt.

Kylie smiled. "I figured as much. I told Allison you wouldn't have ditched us. She really needs friends right about now." She took a slug of her Dr Pepper. "But I do have good news for you." She paused for effect. "I found your cell phone. It was here on your desk in your room the whole time."

"No wonder I couldn't find it."

"Yep, when I tried calling you from here I heard it go off."

We both sat sipping our sodas, listening to the ticking of the kitchen clock. It occurred to me that I should say something about my ride home. If Nick just showed up at our table at school, she would wonder. "Nick Dunstan's going to eat lunch with us on Monday. I invited him." Part of me wanted to tell Kylie about the almost kiss, but it seemed premature, like I might jinx the whole thing if I talked about it too soon.

"That's cool. He's a good guy. Did he tell you that he and Crystal broke up?"

I nodded. "She dumped him for Trey Griffin."

"I don't believe it!"

"Believe it. I got it right from the source."

"Poor Nick." Kylie traced her finger over the lip of the soda can. "And poor, stupid Crystal. She did not choose wisely."

"You know, I'm surprised our talking isn't waking Allison up." I looked in the direction of the living room. Voices carried in my small apartment, not to mention the noise from the people upstairs.

"Allison isn't waking up anytime soon. She took two of something from some prescription she had—Ambien, I think it's called—and like ten minutes later she was dead to the world."

Chapter 19

Morning Has Broken

When I woke up the next morning, I was alone in the living room. The night before I'd opted for the couch, while Kylie slept on the loveseat, a not-too-bad fit for her. The queen-sized air mattress on the floor was all Allison's, since she'd fallen asleep right smack-dab in the middle of it.

Kylie and I'd talked for another hour or so after my arrival home. I asked Kylie if she thought there was any truth to Blake's accusation about the fire at Allison's house.

"No," she said emphatically. "Allison told me she doesn't even remember much about that night, except waking up to smoke and then somehow finding her way outside. She was dizzy and confused, like it was a bad dream. When the fire department came, she realized her parents were still inside. She tried to go back into the house, but the firefighter guys held her back."

"So you don't think she had anything to do with the fire? Maybe even accidentally?"

From the horrified look on Kylie's face I could tell I'd pushed it too far. "Not a chance. If you had seen how she reacted when Blake said she burned down the house, there wouldn't be any doubt in your mind, Rae. Allison's grieving, she's completely wrecked." She blinked back tears. "I can't even imagine what she's going through. She's lost everything."

When my mom came home from the comedy club (well after midnight, I might add), we decided to head for bed. It was too late to fill Gina in on the night's events. Besides I wanted to talk to her in private. I gave her a good-night hug, set up my blankets and pillow on the couch, and fell into a deep sleep.

Now I awoke to the smell of coffee and cigarettes. I heard voices coming from the kitchen. Rubbing my eyes, I listened but couldn't make out the words. Two people talking—one my mom, but I wasn't sure of the other. Finally I was able to place the voice. Allison.

I grabbed my blanket and wrapped it around my shoulders, then trundled into the kitchen.

"Morning, sleepyhead," Gina said, while Allison flashed a thin-lipped smile. It might have been my imagination, but she didn't look too happy to see me. Both of them had coffee in front of them; Allison had both hands wrapped around her mug.

"Good morning. Where's Kylie?"

"Her dad picked her up an hour ago. You were sleeping so soundly we just let you be. She said to tell you she'd call later."

The tile floor was cold against my bare feet. I pulled the blanket more tightly around me.

"We were actually just heading out," my mother said, pushing a piece of paper across the table for me to see. *Rae, Allison and I went to the store. My cell is on. Love, Mom.* At the top of the page she'd put the time: 11:50 a.m. Man, I really did sleep late.

"Why are you going to the store?"

"Allison just needs some things for school." Gina reached over and patted Allison's arm. "Her aunt never seems to get around to it, so I said I'd be glad to help out. It shouldn't take too long. We'll be back in an hour or so."

"Can't I go with you?"

They exchanged a glance, and then Gina said, "Honestly, Rae, we were literally just about to leave. If you were ready to go, I'd say sure, come along, but by the time you take a shower, eat, and get dressed, we'll be back already."

She knew me so well. There was no way I was going anywhere without taking a shower. "Okay," I said, "but don't have any fun without me."

"Never," my mom said, flashing me a smile. She fished in her purse and pulled out her keys. "Ready?" she asked Allison.

I heard them laughing in the hallway as they exited the building. After they left I cleaned up their mess, emptying the ashtray and washing the coffee mugs before I sat down to my bowl of Lucky Charms. I was thinking over the events of last night, and it was then that it hit me—Allison was the only one of us three who hadn't revealed a secret.

Chapter 20

Monday, Monday,
Can't Trust That Day

My mom and Allison returned from shopping with a new backpack and some assorted school supplies. Allison was pretty excited about it, which was good I guess, especially considering her trauma from the night before. After we drove Allison home, we stopped at Taco Bell, always a good thing.

Is it bad that I wasted the rest of Saturday and all of Sunday wishing for Monday? I couldn't stop thinking about Nick, about that brief moment in the car when his lips were against mine. I wondered what would have happened if Kylie hadn't been looking out the window just then. Would he have asked me out for Saturday night? Confessed that he'd secretly liked me for weeks? I envisioned the conversation we might have had, the kissing we would have done. He was so easy to be with—I definitely felt that click that girls always talked about, but I'd never experienced.

On Monday morning, I passed him twice in the halls. The first time he didn't see me. He had his backpack looped over one shoulder and was wearing a gray T-shirt with a skull on the front. With his head down, like he was climbing a hill, I was clearly able to see the adorable spiral cowlick on the crest of his head. The second time I saw him we were going the same direction. I came up from behind and fake-bumped into him. Nick turned and looked irritated until he saw it was me. Then he smiled. "Hey, Rae."

"We're still on for lunch, right?"

"Absolutely."

I would have liked to talk longer, but at that point our schedules reached a crossroads: he went right, and I had to keep going straight. I didn't mind because I knew all I had to do was get through two classes and I'd see him in the cafeteria.

My thoughts of lunch with Nick were interrupted when my name was announced over the loudspeaker in health. "Mrs. Fricker, could you send Rae Maddox down to the office, please?"

The kid behind me poked my back, and predictably, the whole class made that noise, "Oooh…," the one they always made when someone got called down to the office. The assumption was that the one being summoned was in some kind of trouble, and usually that was true. I was hoping, though, that in my case it was Mr. Smedley, relieving me of my Allison duties. I would gladly give up the job.

"Rae?" Mrs. Fricker said, holding out her custom-made hall pass. She'd laminated it onto a wooden paddle. Hard to lose and impossible to duplicate. I took it from her and left my things at my desk. The hour had only just started, and I was sure I wouldn't be gone too long.

Sweet freedom. I felt it walking down the hall, the wooden paddle swinging by my side, and I knew I'd really feel it once Mr. Smedley let me get rid of the Allison noose. I still had her in most of my classes and at lunch, and I'd continue to be friendly, but she wouldn't be my responsibility.

The office lady looked up when I came up to the counter. "Oh good, Rae." I leaned forward and waited for her to tell me I could go right into the vice principal's office, but instead she got up and handed me a slip of paper. "You're all set then, for your dental appointment."

"What?" I looked down at the half sheet in front of me. At the top it said, "Excused Absence." My name and that day's date were listed in the spaces below. Underneath was written: *Dental appointment, teeth cleaning. Will pick up in front of the west entrance at 12:15.* "I think," I said slowly, "there must be some kind of mistake. I don't have an appointment today."

She tsked sympathetically. "This happens more often than you think. A lot of students forget about doctor's visits. Luckily their parents usually remember." Her smile was a little condescending, I thought. "I didn't take the call, Miss Jensen did. She's new, but she's very thorough, always repeats everything back when she takes phone messages. There's no mistake, you'll see."

I was puzzled. Also mystified, baffled, and perplexed. Gina and I had just gone to the dentist not that long ago. At least it seemed like it was recently. Could it have been six months already? I folded the paper and put it in my pocket. Okay then, I was going to the dentist. Having the afternoon off wouldn't be so bad. At least I didn't have any tests scheduled. The good part was that I didn't have to leave until after lunch, so I could still see Nick.

My unexpected dental appointment was still on my mind two hours later when I went into the lunchroom. Kylie and Mason were already at the table. There was no sign of Allison or Nick, but the line for hot lunch was long and I figured they'd catch up to us eventually. I slid in next to Mason and opened my brown paper bag to pull out my stuff: sandwich, Doritos, vitamin water. "Hey, guess what? I get to leave school after lunch."

"I wish I was leaving," Mason said. "I have AP Economics next. Man, I really am not enjoying it."

"You're only a sophomore. Why do you always sign up for those hard classes?" Kylie asked. "They can really kill your GPA if things don't go well."

"I have to. It's family tradition. All the Mihashi boys aim high. It's what we do."

How did we get off the topic of me? "Doesn't anyone even care why I'm leaving early?"

Mason opened a bag of baby carrots. "I care a little bit. Share please." He held a carrot between two fingers like it was a cigar.

"I'm going to the dentist to get my teeth cleaned." I clamped my teeth together and widened my lips so they could get a good view.

"I have never heard anyone so excited about going to the dentist," he said. "You are in serious need of help."

Kylie smiled slyly. "Obviously Rae's oral health is really important to her."

"Stop already," I said. "It's not that I'm excited to go to the dentist, it's that I'm happy to be getting out. My mom never told me about the appointment, but she called it in to the office. This is like a bonus afternoon off. Right after lunch she's going to pick me up at the west door."

"Ah, the west door. That's my favorite one." Mason raised an arm to wave at someone on the other side of the room. I looked up to follow his gesture and saw Nick walking in our direction, holding a tray. "Look lively, Rae. Here comes your boyfriend." He poked me in the side with his elbow. "Heh, heh, heh."

"Shhh…" I gave Kylie, the little blabbermouth, my best dagger look. She just laughed.

"Is this seat taken?" Nick asked. He motioned to the spot next to me, then sat down before I could answer.

"I was saving it just for you." Man, I was bold. He nodded and grinned. There was definitely something going on between us. I just wasn't sure what yet.

Allison walked up then and slid wordlessly next to Kylie on the opposite side of the table. Kylie put half her sandwich on a napkin and slid it over to share. "Thanks, Allison. Here Rae has a guy on either side of her, and I'm sitting all by myself. I'm glad *someone* wants to sit next to me."

"Yeah, I don't know why everyone is always avoiding you," Mason said. "Your scabies are hardly noticeable anymore." He leaned forward and extended a hand to Nick. "Welcome to our little group. There aren't many of us, but we're all cool." Honestly, Mason was such a geek. Really funny at times, but still a geek.

They shook hands in the space in front of my chest, and then Nick said, "Glad to be here." He released his grip and sat back. "I'd like to thank Rae for inviting me. If not for her, I would have been table-less today. A very sad thing."

Allison came to attention. "Why aren't you at Blake's table?"

Nick made a slicing gesture across his throat. "I was banished."

"Why were you banished?" Allison asked.

"Because I'm not going out with Crystal anymore. I thought they were my friends. Turns out, I was wrong."

"They actually said you couldn't eat lunch with them?" Kylie asked.

"Not in so many words. I figured it out when no one would talk to me all morning."

Allison tipped her head in that direction. "So what would happen if you went over there right now and sat down with them?"

Nick shrugged. "They wouldn't body slam me, if that's what you're getting at. I could probably sit there if I wanted to, but I don't want to."

There was a long silence, the only noise the sound of Mason crunching on carrots.

"Well, who wants friends like that anyway?" Kylie said, looking around the table, and we all nodded in agreement.

"That happens a lot," Allison said, her tone serious. "People you care about turn on you, and then you're on your own. You don't think it will happen, but it does."

I sat up straight, startled by her words. Could she mean me? Did she know I'd been hiding in the bushes at Blake's bonfire and hadn't come to help her? I had to know. "Are you talking about one of us?"

"Oh no," Allison shook her head. "You guys are the best. I don't know where I'd be without you. It was at my other school, before I came here. I went through something when my parents died, and no one would believe me—" She blinked back tears, her voice breaking. "None of my friends would talk to me."

Kylie handed Allison a napkin for her eyes and put an arm around her shoulders. I could tell from looking at Mason and Nick's faces that they knew Allison's story. The guys looked uncomfortable at her show of emotion, and I was sympathetic, but once again, I didn't know what to say.

"You don't have to worry about that here," Kylie said firmly. "You're safe with us. We don't let our friends down."

To break the tension, the rest of the lunch hour was spent expanding on this concept. Kylie made a small flag using a fruit snack wrapper and a straw and embedded it in a marshmallow she found on the floor. It represented new territory, she said. There was some talk of a blood oath (Mason), but the rest of us thought that was kind of extreme. "The main thing," Allison said, "is that we're here for each other no matter what."

I knew they were half-joking, but still, it was the most intense lunch hour I'd ever had in a high school cafeteria. I hoped it wouldn't scare Nick off. I liked having him next to me, watching him as he ate and talked. He had an easy confidence without being too full of himself. I could use some of that myself.

The bell rang as we were cleaning up our wrappers and napkins. Mason gave a salute as he stood up to go. "Off to economics. Have fun at the dentist, Rae."

"You're going to the dentist?" Nick said.

"Yep, my mom called it in. I didn't know anything about it until I got called down to the office for my pass. It was like— surprise!" I did jazz hands. "You're getting your teeth cleaned today."

We were the only ones left at the table now, but neither of us was making a move to go. "I've always felt that clean teeth are really important," he said. "That and really fresh breath are an unbeatable combination."

He made it sound so personal. Could it be he was flirting using dental metaphors? The boy was impressive. "I feel strongly about that too," I said.

"Rae, can I call you tonight? We could talk more about this teeth issue."

"I'd like that." Look at me grinning like an idiot and opening up to another human being. It was easier than I would have thought.

"Can I have your cell number?"

"Oh sure." I dug into my backpack and pulled out a sheet of paper, then wrote down my number and name. My hand was shaking a little. I hoped he wouldn't notice.

"Thank you very much." He looked at the paper. "Rae Mad-dox. Good to have the name so I don't think I'm calling some other girl."

I blushed, which I almost never do, but how stupid was that, putting down my full name? I just wasn't completely sure he knew it, and I thought this would be a subtle way of telling him.

"I'll talk to you tonight." He looked around the mostly empty lunchroom. "I guess I should get going. Don't want to be late for class."

"Yeah, and I really shouldn't keep the dentist waiting."

Chapter 21

It's Not Always
What You Expect

I stood looking out the west door at exactly 12:15, the excused absence slip in hand. I'd been ready to show it to anyone who questioned my leaving midday, but no one did. In fact, the office lady saw me and waved as I went by. *Good-bye, Rae, wherever you're going!* The building was not nearly as secure as they'd have us believe.

Ten minutes later, still standing there, I looked remarkably like someone whose mother had screwed up royally. She could be so lax about time; I hoped she wasn't going to make me late. I stepped outside and got out my cell phone. Inside the building it was difficult to get a clear signal, but now that I was outdoors there was nothing between me and the satellite but some clouds and an American flag flapping against the aluminum pole.

I pushed the button to turn it on, but before I could call, a car pulled up directly in front of me. Not my mom's Saturn, but a large silver SUV. I took a step back as the passenger side window slowly opened. "Rae Maddox?" It was Blake Daly.

"Yeah?"

"Get in. I'm your ride."

I leaned in to look at him eye-level. "Get out of here. I'm waiting for my mom. She's a little late, but she'll be here any minute."

"She's not coming," Blake said. "I'm the one who called in for you. Get in."

WTF? "No, my mom—"

"There's no dentist appointment. I made that up so I could take you somewhere and show you something."

"What are you talking about?"

"It's about Allison. If you really want to help her, get in the car."

He had to be kidding. "No, I'm not getting in your car. If you have something to tell me, just tell me already."

"It's not that simple. Now look." He pointed behind me. "That annoying woman from the office is coming. You better get in, or you're going to get both of us in trouble." The window slowly rose upward.

"Rae?" Miss Jensen opened the outer door and stuck her head out. "Is there a problem?"

"No problem," I said. "Just leaving for my dentist appointment."

She showed no signs of leaving until I actually got into the car, so I did, waving as I opened the door to reassure her everything was fine. Blake drove off before I'd even fastened my seat belt. When we were a block away I said, "Would you please pull over and tell me what in the hell is going on?"

He eased the car curbside. Down the block I saw an old guy raking his leaves, but he didn't seem to notice us. "I already told you what's going on." Blake drummed his fingers against the steering wheel. "What else do you need to know, Maddox?"

"You didn't tell me what's going on. Words came out of your mouth, but they made no sense to me. You were the one who called in my excused absence? How did that work?"

"I do it all the time. I called in and said I was your dad and I was calling in because you forgot the note at home. It was easy."

"I don't even have a dad."

He shrugged. "They don't know that. If you call at a busy time, they just write it down. They didn't have a clue. I made sure to spell your name the way an annoying middle-aged guy would. I said, 'Maddox—M as in Michael, A, double D as in doctor—'"

"Yeah I get it," I said. "And *why* did you call in and say you were my dad?"

"I told you, because I want to take you somewhere that will give you some insights into Allison. She's your friend, right? And you want to help her, don't you?"

I wouldn't exactly call her a friend, but the fact that I didn't categorize her that way was no reflection on Allison; it was more of a Rae thing. Not taking on friends too easily was basic self-protection. Still, I was warming up to Allison, and I *did* feel for her. I wanted to help, but somehow I doubted that Blake's motives were pure. "What if they call my mother to confirm my absence?"

"Won't happen," he said. "They've already issued the pass. It would make them look bad if they found out it was bogus."

"What if I get out of this car right now and walk back to school, tell them what you did?"

"You could do that." He looked amused. "But I don't think you will. You're too smart for that. It would just get both of us in trouble, and then you'd never know what I was going to show you."

Chapter 22

All in Your Head

"So where are we going?" I asked.

"You'll see when we get there."

"Can you give me a clue? Is it even in Wisconsin? Are we driving out of state?"

"Chill. It's just a few blocks from here."

I shouldn't have been surprised when he pulled up in front of the building also known as the Mental Health Unit for Children and Adolescents, but somehow I was. It looked the same as always, a giant brick with windows.

"Do you know where we are?" Blake raised his eyebrows; his tone was smug.

"Yeah," I said. "This is the Mental Health Unit for Children and Adolescents, also known as the children's division of the psychiatric hospital. Personally, I like to call it Mother HUCA." I could tell I surprised him; the superior look left his face. "And yes, I do know that Allison was a resident here."

"She told you that?" he asked incredulously.

"I know a lot of things."

"Well," he said, taking the key out of the ignition, "let's see what else you know."

He got out of the car and headed down the sidewalk. When I didn't get out fast enough, he turned around and gestured for me to follow. I had to hurry to catch up. He took long strides and headed down a path to the left of the fence. We circled around the building until we came to what had to be the main door. It didn't look very main though—just a regular-sized door with a metal canopy over it. Blake pressed a button on a box next to the doorframe, and a woman's voice came over an intercom. "Good afternoon, what's the reason for your visit?"

"This is Blake Daly. I have a twelve o'clock appointment with Dr. Winfield."

Okay, this I did not know.

She buzzed us in, and Blake led the way toward a large desk near the entrance. The woman sitting there said, "Hi, Blake," and handed him a clipboard. He wrote his name and mine on the sheet, and under the column that asked "reason for visit" he wrote "appointment with Dr. Winfield / guest." I didn't know if I was supposed to be his guest or the guest of the facility. Either way wasn't too thrilling for me.

He handed the clipboard back to the woman and motioned for me to follow him down a long hallway.

"Am I ever going to find out what this is about?" I asked as we walked.

"Soon enough." He stopped in front of the last door on the left. A sign holder on the wall next to the door read: *Quiet please. In session.* "We have to wait."

"Don't you have to live here to see the doctors? I thought this was just for the resident kids."

He shrugged. "I don't know how it works. My family had to start coming here because of Allison. I never even heard of this place before."

I was having serious doubts about this whole thing. The locked doors, the writing of my name on the sign-in sheet, me missing a half-day of school. How had this happened? I used to be smarter than this. I was the one who moved on when situations got sticky. My policy was to never get bogged down in other people's problems. Was it too late to walk out? I could make it home on foot in ten minutes and just hang out there all afternoon. If Gina were home, I'd tell her the truth. We'd have a good laugh about it, I was sure of that. But what if she asked why I didn't just stay and find out more about what Allison was going through? I was here now; maybe I should just stay.

Before I had a chance to anguish over it any longer, the door opened and a boy about eight, wearing a baseball cap, bounced out. Behind him, a trim woman with dark curly hair called out, "Okay, Caleb, see you next week then."

"See you next week then," he echoed, grinning. Such a happy boy. Whatever his problem was I'd take two of them.

She turned to us. "Ah, Blake and friend. Come on in."

Friend? I had gotten promoted from disliked acquaintance to friend in no time at all. If I didn't watch it, by spring we'd be going to prom together.

Blake did the introductions. "Dr. Winfield, this is Rae. Rae, the doc."

Nice. We shook hands, and she motioned for us to sit. Her office had the traditional desk along with a sitting area consisting of two chairs and a couch. Beyond the desk was an area set up for little kids: a small table and chairs, a bookcase filled with toys, a dollhouse on the window ledge. The room smelled good, like gingerbread. I sat in one of the chairs, and Dr. Winfield sat at the other, a notebook on her lap. Blake sat back on the couch as comfortably as if he were at home watching a Packer game.

"I'm not really sure why I'm here," I said. "Blake said it was something about Allison?"

Dr. Winfield stiffened. "Blake, you know I can't legally or ethically discuss anyone besides you."

Blake laughed nervously. "Well, I had to say something to get her to come, right?"

She turned to me. "I'm sure you've heard of physician-patient privilege. It's intended to protect the rights of patients, and I abide by it."

Blake said, "I know, Doc, but we can talk about me, right? And how having Allison at my house is affecting me?"

She nodded. "We can talk about you, and Rae, as your friend, is free to join in the conversation."

"I'm not really his friend."

She raised her eyebrows. "No?"

"I barely know Blake. He said if I came I'd find out more about Allison and that I'd be able to help her."

The doctor tapped her fingertips together. "You were misled, I think, and so was I. Blake told me that he was bringing a friend who wanted to help him with what he's going through." We both looked at Blake, who grinned sheepishly.

"Hey, whatever works, huh? Allison *is* my problem, and my mom said Rae is the one person she's connected with. You said that if someone could break through Allison's ice queen act you could get her the help she needs, and then she could move in with her other relatives in Iowa."

Dr. Winfield's lips formed a thin line. "So that's what this is about, Blake? Getting rid of Allison?"

"She can't keep living with us." He ran his fingers through his hair. "My parents expect me to take her places with my friends. I can't do that. You never know when she'll start crying about nothing. I can't handle it. Honestly, I think she'd be better off living somewhere else."

"Maybe," I said, "she wouldn't cry so much if you weren't so mean to her."

That got his attention. "Okay, I know she told you what I said at the bonfire. I admit it was really mean to say she killed her parents, but I didn't know she was there, or I wouldn't have said it." He leaned back. "It's the truth, though. Even the cops up north think she burned down her own house. And another thing," he said, pointing at me, "if she tells you no one in my family cares about her, that's just wrong. My mom has tried everything to help Allison, and still she won't talk to any of us. Just because she's spilled her guts to you doesn't mean she's said shit to anyone else."

I raised a hand. "May I just say that Allison hasn't opened up to me at all? She barely talks to me. If anything, she's more friendly to Kylie and Mason and my mom."

"Your mom?" Dr. Winfield held her pen poised over the notebook. "Is your mother a very nurturing, maternal type?"

Not hardly. "She's nice," I said cautiously. "Very nice. Everyone likes her. She takes an interest in people."

She turned to Blake. "Just for the record, and I'm speaking in generalities here, I never make promises about the children and teenagers I see in my practice. Each person is unique, as is their life and their progress in dealing with whatever problems they have. I would never say, for example, that if X happens, then Y will be done. If you somehow got that impression from something I said, I am sorry. That was never my intent."

Blake looked bewildered. His jock brain was overloaded.

"She's saying," I translated, "that she never promised that if Allison made progress she could move out of your house and live somewhere else."

"No," he said, "that's not right. My mom said if Allison admitted she set the fire, you'd have to take her back here to live. And that after that she could move out of state."

"Maybe this is something we can discuss at your family's next session," Dr. Winfield said. "*This* isn't the appropriate time with Rae here."

I picked my backpack up off the floor. "That's okay, I have to get going anyway. I have this thing I'm supposed to be at."

Chapter 23

Calling in Reinforcements

So I headed for home, thinking about Allison the whole way. How awful it must be to live with Blake, who didn't hide the fact that he didn't want her there. I couldn't even imagine how that felt. Every time my mom told the story of my birth, she made it clear how excited she was to have me, how much she loved me.

Starting when I was three or four, she used to tease me by pretending not to know me. If I woke up during the night, I'd come into her bedroom, where she, night owl that she was, would be watching TV or reading a magazine. "What's this?" she'd say in delight. "There's a little girl in my bedroom!" I'd laugh and snuggle up next to her. She'd cup my chin and look me right in the eye. "You know, you look *exactly* like someone I love," she'd say, and I'd squeal, "I *am* someone you love."

She did that for years, until I wouldn't play along anymore.

When I got home, I let myself into our apartment and called out, "Mom?" even though her Saturn wasn't in the lot. Sometimes she let friends use the car. But there was no answer, and I remembered she was scheduled to work nine to three that day.

I set my backpack down and poured myself some apple-mango juice. Actually, the label said it was apple-mango fruit drink, which accounted for its unnatural color and sweet Kool-Aid-ish taste. Still, it hit the spot. With a bag of Doritos, I could consume all of the required food group chemicals at one sitting.

I was crunching, sipping, crunching, sipping when the phone rang. I picked up on the second ring. Hearing my grandma's voice immediately brightened my afternoon. "Rae, darling girl, what a nice surprise. I was thinking I'd get the machine."

"I have the afternoon off of school. I just came back from an appointment."

"Nothing's wrong, I hope."

"Nope, just got my teeth cleaned." Say it enough times and it feels like the truth. "So, Grandma, how are you?" My grandparents rarely called my mom because it pissed her off if they did it too often. She felt they were trying to manipulate her. She didn't know I talked to them on my cell phone at least once a week. I relied on their calls. They kept me grounded.

"I'm good," she said and then filled me in on their most recent activities. They'd just re-roofed the house, there was a potluck dinner at their church—everyone raved about Grandma's lasagna—and Grandpa's arthritis was giving him some grief so they'd installed a hot tub on the deck. "For therapeutic reasons," Grandma emphasized. This was the kind of thing that would have killed Gina. She'd say it was so Midwestern of them to have to justify every luxury.

"But here's the reason I'm really calling," she said. "My sister Dorothy and her husband Bill are here visiting from Florida, and I thought it would be so nice if you and your mom came down for the weekend." My heart leapt and then sank. I ached to see them, but I also knew my mom wouldn't go for it. "We'll make a vacation out of it." She was campaigning now. "Go out to eat, maybe drive down to Chicago and see a show on Sunday. Grandpa said he could order matinee tickets to see the Blue Man Group on Sunday, if you want."

"That sounds great," I said. "But I'm pretty sure my mom works this weekend." Mom used the work excuse often to avoid them. If you didn't know better, you'd think her job was as important as an emergency room doctor or a homicide detective.

"You don't have to give me an answer right now." Grandma's voice sounded less hopeful. "Talk to your mom and get back to me."

I said I would.

"And Rae," she added, "if your mother can't make it, maybe she'll let us have you for the weekend. Grandpa would be glad to come and pick you up." They were less than an hour away, after all. So close and yet so far.

After I'd hung up the phone, I cleaned up my Doritos crumbs, rinsed out my glass, and then headed out the door to Studio 64, the salon where my mom worked. She was more likely to say yes to any request when other people were around. With any luck, I'd be spending the next weekend in Madison.

Chapter 24
Snooty 64

Studio 64 was located in a strip mall that also housed a gourmet wine and cheese store, a specialty bakery, a teeth-whitening boutique, and an upscale dress shop called Martina's. The shop carried sequined tops for four hundred dollars and dresses that cost triple that. Rumor had it that Oprah had been spotted in Martina's with relatives who lived in the area, but Gina had never met anyone who had actually seen her there.

The salon was by far the most high-class place my mom had ever worked. In the past, her salons had names like Shear Delight and Bonnie's Cut and Curl. Sometimes she was the only manicurist. One place, Big Jean's Beauty Palace, I remembered fondly because they'd let me come in with my mom on my days off school. I'd help by sweeping, straightening the magazines, and taking out the trash. The customers gave me loose change as tips, and predicted a promising career for me in the beauty business. I was about seven or eight at the time, and Big Jean's felt like my second home. If it had been up to me, I would have stayed in that small town in Arkansas forever.

Gina felt that Studio 64 was the ultimate, the top of the employment ladder. The clientele was upper class and tipped accordingly. The only problem so far, she said, was her micromanaging control-freak boss, Francine. It was always something.

I paused at the front desk where Ashley, the nice receptionist, talked on the phone while entering something on the computer. She smiled and waved me toward the area in back.

When I walked into her cubicle, my mom got a huge grin on her face. "Rae!" she cried out. She got up and gave me a hug, then pulled a chair over for me. "Sasha, this is my daughter, Rae."

"So nice to finally meet you," Sasha said. Impeccably dressed in business attire and pearl earrings, she looked like a news anchor. "Your mother is always bragging about you and your good grades. No classes today?"

"It was a half day." This lying thing got easier each time. "I got out after lunch."

Gina nodded. She could never keep track of my school schedule.

"I'm sorry to interrupt," I said, "but we got an important phone call from Grandma." My mother rolled her eyes, but I continued anyway. "She wanted to know if we could come down for the weekend." I filled her in on all the details while she applied crimson polish to Sasha's nails.

Gina looked irked. "We're not going to be dropping everything to go running down to Madison on a moment's notice. For one thing, I have to work on Saturday. And afterward I have plans for the evening."

"I thought you might be scheduled to work, but Grandma said if that was the case I could just come by myself. Grandpa would drive up and get me."

Gina stopped to address Sasha. "Isn't this exactly what I was telling you about?"

Sasha nodded sympathetically. "Mine are the same way. If they can't control you, they'll go right for the kids. It's so underhanded."

Gina sighed. "We'll talk about this when I get home, Rae."

This wasn't looking good for me. "It's just that I haven't seen them since we moved here, and they're so close now—"

"I said we'd talk about it later." Her voice was steady, and the look she gave me could have cut through glass.

The unfairness of it hit me solidly. Just because she was mad at them, I had to suffer? "You're just going to say no. Admit it." I stood up, and my chair scraped loudly against the tile. "You never give them a chance. You're so full of yourself, you automatically assume everything Grandma and Grandpa do is aimed at controlling you." I was getting louder, but I didn't care. "Maybe they just want to see us—is that so hard to understand?"

"Keep. Your. Voice. Down." Gina held the nail polish brush midair. Sasha looked down at the table. "I said we'd discuss this at home."

"I'm not going home," I yelled. It came out without any thought, pure reflex on my part. I turned on my heel and rushed out of the salon, pushing past the owner, Francine, who came to see what all the commotion was about. I saw her curious, frowning face and the way the other customers lifted their heads to watch as I ran out, but I didn't look back. I had to get out of there.

Chapter 25

Now What?

The problem with making a dramatic exit is that sometimes you say things that just screw yourself. I couldn't be at the apartment when my mom got home. And yet, where was I going to go?

My timing was off. If it were a little earlier, I could have caught Mason or Kylie on their way out of school and rode the bus home with them. Once I was at their house, I could have left a message for Gina saying I was spending the evening with a friend and I'd be home by eight. By the time I got back things would have cooled down, and we could have talked calmly. This whole thing was her fault. If only she wasn't so impossible when it came to my grandparents.

The weather wasn't cooperating either—a little on the chilly side. Autumn was a fooler with its beautiful leaves, apple harvest, and pumpkin farm hayrides. Sweatshirt weather, Grandma called it. Football season, was Grandpa's take on it. But to me it was the death of summer.

I stepped off the curb and headed away from the strip mall. Walking was so overrated. Once I got my driver's license and had my own car, I was never walking anywhere again. Except maybe through parking lots to get to my car.

I flipped open my phone to look at the time. Quarter to three. Yep, my guess was right. Kylie and Mason would already be on the bus, not walking aimlessly like some people. Lucky them.

I closed my phone and it rang, or, to be precise, I should say it started playing "We're Not Going to Take It" by Twisted Sister. Sometimes eighties music was a perfect fit. "Hello?"

"Hey, Rae." It was Nick. He sounded happy. "Are you all through with the dentist?"

"I'm all through with everyone." To counteract the bitterness of my words, I laughed a little.

"That doesn't include me, I hope."

"No. You would be the exception."

And that was how I wound up riding in Nick's truck on what turned out to be a beautiful autumn afternoon after all. I gave him my coordinates, the corner of Oakland Road and Petrie Street, and he came and picked me up. Seeing Nick's pickup driving toward me was a beautiful sight.

"So," he said, once I got my seat belt clicked into place, "any cavities that need drilling?"

"Ha! Just one. His name is Blake." I found myself telling him all about my afternoon—from Blake calling in for me, right up until my blow-up at the Studio 64 salon. "And the worst part is I know she won't let me go see my grandparents. When we moved here I thought I'd get to see them all the time since we're so close, but my mother has such issues with them they might as well be across the country."

He whistled. "Quite an afternoon you've had, Ms. Maddox. Sounds like you could use a distraction."

"Are you offering?"

"Yes, I am."

He pulled away from the curb, and I didn't even ask where we were going. It was nice to let someone else take care of things.

Sitting in the passenger seat, I could look at him without feeling like a creepy stalker. He glanced my way and smiled, and I flashed one back. How was it that one week ago he was Crystal Light's boyfriend, and now here I sat in her spot and it didn't feel weird at all?

"Don't you wonder where I'm taking you?" he asked.

"Somewhere far away, I hope."

He laughed. "Not too far. But you'll like it, I think."

We turned off the main street and onto the highway. I watched as we drove past clusters of new subdivisions and headed toward wide-open spaces—farm fields and meadows.

"Big sky country," I observed, quoting my grandfather. I think it really applied to cattle ranches out west, but he used it anytime we were away from the city.

"My neck of the woods." Nick pointed. "I live just ahead on the left."

A sign along the road showed the outline of an apple with the words "Dunstan Orchards." We drove past it and turned onto a long unpaved driveway, the truck's wheels perfectly aligned with the ruts in the dirt. Ahead I saw a white farmhouse and behind that, a red barn. "Your family has an apple orchard?"

"Yeah, it's been our family business for four generations." He grinned. "This time of year we're all about the apples." He parked the truck, and we walked up the path to the enclosed porch. He opened the door and walked through, holding it open for me to follow. "My mom's car is gone. She must be out making deliveries."

Inside the screened porch, a large note was tacked to the inside door. *Nick, 2 Honeycrisp, 4 Jonathan, 3 McIntosh. Love, Mom.*

This, he explained, is what he came home to every day during apple season. The orchard used to be a full-scale operation, but his family had sold off most of the land over the years. His father worked as an engineer, and he and his mother did the apples in the fall. "When my brother and sister were at home, we had a roadside stand," he said, "but once they went off to college, we lost half our labor force. Now Mom just takes orders over the phone. She delivers for a fee. Sometimes people knock at the door and want to do the pick-your-own thing, and we're cool with that."

I snuck a glance around the porch, taking note of the white wicker furniture with floral cushions. A large orange tabby slept on the chair closest to us, and Nick reached down and stroked its belly as he talked.

Four generations of Dunstans had lived in this house, this warm, cozy place. Year after year, Nick's family walked up the steps to the porch, celebrated Thanksgiving in the same kitchen, watched the sun set over the same horizon. While I, on the other hand, was lucky to finish two years in one school. It seemed that Nick Dunstan had gotten the childhood I'd always wanted.

"So, are you ready to pick apples?"

"We're picking apples?"

He held up his mom's note. "Two bushels of Honeycrisp, four of Jonathan, and three of McIntosh."

I waited in the truck while he went and got nets and empty bushel baskets from the barn. I had no idea how someone picked apples, other than just reaching up and pulling, like Dorothy did in *The Wizard of Oz*. Come to think of it, that strategy didn't go so well for her.

Nick gave me a crash course in apples. He drove underneath the appropriate tree, and then we stood on the bed of the truck and used the metal teeth on the inside rim of the nets to pull down the apples. We filled each bushel until it was full to the brim and went on to the next. It was surprisingly fun. I wasn't cold anymore—moving around seemed to fix that—and we talked and laughed as we worked. He told me that Crystal's friends had come out to the orchard once to help, but they lost interest right away and started throwing apples at each other. "Bunch of idiots," he said.

As the bushels multiplied at our feet, there was less space for us to maneuver. When we bumped backsides, he said, "Whoa, we were cheek to cheek there for a second." I blushed but didn't say anything, and he held up an apple. "Your face is as red as this." He moved closer and looped an arm around my waist and held the apple next to my cheek. "Exactly this color." I didn't say anything. I could feel my heart pounding and my entire body tingling. I didn't have much experience in this department, but instinctively I moved toward him until we were pressed together.

Before I knew it, we were sitting and then lying down, our legs overlapping and our lips doing the same. We were making out like crazy, only pulling apart to look at each other in wonder like *I can't believe this is happening.* "I'm so glad it's you," he said at one point, touching his forehead to mine. His words didn't quite make sense, but I knew exactly what he meant because I felt the same way. I'd always thought that girls who did this kind of thing were a little on the slutty side. Sitting in my room at night, giving the subject of relationships careful thought, I'd always thought the smart thing to do was start slow, meet for coffee, or go out for burgers. Maybe the first time there'd be a goodnight kiss or some hand holding. I never imagined I'd be lying in the back of a pickup truck, apples rolling against my head, not caring about anything but Nick Dunstan and the moment.

I could have gone on like that forever. I could have lived in the back of the truck, subsisting on Nick and his apples and the autumn breeze on my face. If my phone hadn't rung, we'd be there still, I think. But my phone did go off, the very loud strains of "We're Not Going to Take It" ruining the moment.

"Nice ring tone." He smirked, a look I usually hated, it was so smartass-ish, but on him it worked—totally cool.

I sat up and smoothed the front of my sweatshirt, then pulled out my phone. It was my mother. "Hi, Mom."

"Hello, Rae." Oh, but she was furious. Her pissed-off tone gave it all away. "Were you planning on coming home sometime soon? Or are you going to stay mad over nothing forever?"

I ran my fingers through my hair. "I'm not mad. I just went to a friend's house. I meant to call. I guess I forgot. I'm sorry." I shot a look at Nick and rolled my eyes.

She ranted a bit more about me making a scene where she worked. Her boss was not pleased, she said. "And where are you, anyway? Which friend?"

"Um, I'm at Nick Dunstan's house."

"I don't think I've met anyone named Nick. Are either of his parents home?" Now I knew she was really mad. This was the kind of question other people's mothers asked, not mine.

"No, I don't think his parents are home."

Nick shook his head and held out his hand. "Let me talk to her."

I reluctantly handed him the phone.

"Ms. Maddox?" I watched as he put his head in the lion's mouth voluntarily. "This is Nick Dunstan. My parents own an apple orchard on Highway 47, and Rae is just helping me pick apples. I hope that's okay."

There was a long pause before she answered. I couldn't make out the words.

"You're right. She should have called. I take full responsibility for that. We had a pretty big order to fill today, and we got so caught up filling the bushels I think it slipped both our minds."

More sounds from my mother's end, but softer this time.

"Okay, sure," he said. "I understand. No problem. I'm looking forward to meeting you too." He handed the phone back to me.

"Pretty slick maneuver having him cover for you." She'd lost her edge, defeated by Nick Dunstan's charm. "I told your friend to bring you home. It's important. We really need to talk."

Chapter 26
Turn and Face the Strain

The ride home was way too short. I was quiet most of the way, anticipating my mother's "talk." Any time she phrased it that way it was something big. I didn't think it was just about me going to Nick's without calling first.

Was she planning on cutting all off all ties with my grandparents? She always threatened to do that, but every Christmas we went back—me because I liked seeing them, and Gina to collect the envelope filled with cash. I didn't know why she couldn't talk to her own parents. Why not just clear the air and tell them she was still suffering from the time they'd had her committed? It seemed easy enough, but whenever I mentioned it she shut me down. Just like the subject of my father, the matter was off limits.

Maybe it wasn't even about Grandma and Grandpa this time. Maybe she was just mad at me for causing a ruckus at the salon. If she was pissed about that, it would be easy enough to fix. I'd apologize nonstop for a day or two, and then we'd move on. That's the way it always worked.

I hated not knowing what was going on in her head.

"You're awfully quiet," Nick said as he pulled in front of my building.

"I'm not looking forward to this. My mom doesn't get mad very often, but when she does, look out."

"It'll be okay." He gave me a reassuring smile. "Really."

Easy for him to say—Mr. Lived-in-the-same-house-for-four-generations. I knew he was trying to make me feel better though, so I smiled back as if I agreed.

Now that we were on my turf, it was my turn to lead the way. I unlocked the outer door and took him through the front hallway, past the wall-mounted mailbox slots and the scuffed walls, to apartment 1A. "Mom?" I called out as we entered. "I'm home."

The TV was on in her bedroom. I heard it click off, and she came out to where we stood in the living room. "Hello," she said, holding out her hand, "you must be Nick."

I always found meeting other people's parents awkward, but Nick had all the right moves. He shook her hand and introduced himself, first and last name, and then he apologized for getting me home so late. His fault, he said. Then he produced one perfect apple from his pocket—a Honeycrisp—and said I'd been a big help picking apples at the orchard. If she'd tell him her favorite kind of apple, he'd bring a bushel next time.

"Oh, that's not really necessary," she said. I knew she was wondering what in the hell she'd do with a bushel of apples. There was no pie baking or cider pressing at our apartment. We bought apples two at a time, and even then they sometimes went bad. "As long as Rae promises to call next time, we're good."

There was an air of finality to the way she stood, one hand on hip. I could tell she wanted him to go, and he must have felt it too because he said, "Well, my mom must be wondering where I am, so I better be going. See you tomorrow, Rae." His smile was like a secret between us. It spoke of the kiss we would have exchanged if Gina weren't standing right there.

After he left she said, "He seems nice," in a kind of snarky way. I didn't say anything, so she went one further. "So, apple picking? Is that what the kids are calling it nowadays?"

"We *were* apple picking."

"Were you lying in the tree when you were doing it?" She reached over and pulled something out of my hair. A leaf. Oops. "The back of your sweatshirt is dirty too."

"He uses his truck for hauling. I must have picked up some of it on the drive home." I lifted the bottom edge of my hoodie and gave it a shake, but whatever was on there wasn't coming off. I looked up and met her eyes. "We were going to have a big talk?"

She turned serious. "You're lucky I'm not going to give you holy hell for your little performance at the salon. Don't even think of pulling that crap again, Rae."

"Okay, sorry."

"The reason I'm letting you off easy is because your little stunt pissed off Francine and she read me the riot act, which forced me to do some serious thinking." She tapped her forehead to illustrate exactly where her serious thinking was done. "Do I want to work for someone so evil? No, I do not. So, after much thought, I have a new game plan for us. You might not like it initially, but in the end I think it will be for the best."

"Oh God no." I put my hand over my mouth; I suddenly felt sick.

"Don't get so weirded out." Gina reached over and squeezed my shoulder. "No one died. Why don't you wait here—I'll get us something to drink, and we can talk."

I knew it—she wanted to move. I sat down numbly and looked around the living room. It wasn't the greatest apartment, but I'd gotten used to it. When I woke up at night I could find my way to the bathroom without turning on the light. I had friends now, better friends than I'd had at other schools. And now I had Nick. It was just a beginning, but with him I felt a connection. It was the start of something great, I could tell. Looking ahead I saw us as a couple, going to prom together, talking on the phone every night. I'd never thought *not* having a boyfriend was any big deal, but I'd been fooling myself.

This always happened. I just started to find my way in a place, and before I could take it any farther, we were gone. Grandpa said Gina thrived on change and chaos. When the going gets tough, Gina gets going, he said. Boy, did he have her number.

I was sick of change and chaos. Sick of making new friends and learning the ins and outs of yet another school. I just wanted everything to stay the same for once.

She came back a few minutes later with mugs of hot chocolate with whipped cream on top. The kind of thing that would have won me over when I was, say, ten. Here I was, fifteen, and we were still in the same routine.

"Please do not say we're moving." I gave her a serious look. "We've only been here for a few months. We can't keep doing this."

She took a sip. "Ooh, that's hot—be careful."

"You know how important high school is. How am I ever going to get into college if my transcripts are from all over the place?"

"I knew you'd be like this. I understand how you feel, but let's just look at it from my point of view for a minute, okay?" She raised her eyebrows and set the mug down on the coffee table. "You knew from the start that I've always hated Wisconsin. I only agreed to move here because of the job opportunity and so that you'd be closer to Grandma and Grandpa."

Both of them half-truths—she'd really moved here to follow her boyfriend at the time, Dave Somebody. As soon as we moved, he'd ended things. But I wasn't going to be the one to bring that up.

"But now," she continued, "the job isn't going so well. The kicker was, and I don't hold you responsible for this, so don't worry, that that bitch Francine reamed me a new asshole in front of a customer. She had a meltdown after you left the salon. She said your behavior made me look unprofessional and that it reflected poorly on the salon."

"You were fired?" My throat was sawdust. This was worse than I thought.

"No, and I didn't quit, either. Don't think I didn't want to." Gina pointed a finger in my direction. "You would have been very proud of me, Rae. I just listened politely and apologized, even though it killed me. I just kept thinking about how upset Allison would be if we left right now. I just know she would feel completely abandoned. She already has trust issues. I need to give her some notice—"

"How upset *Allison* would be?" The words exploded out of me. "You're unbelievable! What about me, your daughter?" I stood up. "Don't you even care about how you're destroying *my* life?"

Gina frowned. "Just calm down," she said sharply. "If you'd let me finish, we could actually discuss this."

I sat down. My heart was hammering, and I felt a little shaky. "Okay, go ahead—discuss."

"What I was about to say is that I didn't make a rash decision like I usually do." She took another sip from her mug. "I thought things through for once."

"Good." I crossed my arms in front of me.

"Despite how nasty Francine is, I think I can stick out the job a little longer—say to the end of the semester? Then you can finish your sophomore year at the new place, and wherever we live next we'll stay for your junior and senior year, I promise."

"Yeah, just like you promised we'd stay here until I graduated from high school."

She held up a hand like stopping traffic. "Neither of us likes the cold weather, right? So I'm thinking someplace south, but not too humid in the summer. You can research it on the Internet. I'll even let you pick out the place, as long as there are jobs available there."

I could tell by her big grin that I was supposed to like this plan. "If I'm picking the place, I vote to stay here until the end of my senior year. There are other jobs in the area. Why don't you just get one at another salon?"

Her face fell. "Rae, be reasonable. You know that once I quit a job I don't stick around. You make friends very easily, you always have. My philosophy is if you've made a mistake, just cut your losses and move on, and Wisconsin is clearly a mistake for me. I don't want to get into it, but this place brings back a lot of bad memories for me. A lot of bad memories."

"What memories would those be? Something to do with my father? Are you afraid you'll run into him at the mall?"

I'd struck a nerve. She set her mug down hard; hot chocolate sloshed over the rim and onto the coffee table. "This conversation is over," she said, standing up. "I tried to let you have some say in this, but you're not even trying. It's really not up to you, Rae, it never has been. I'm the one who makes the money, so I decide what's best." She got up and went into her bedroom and closed and locked the door.

In the aftermath of her outburst, I did what I always did: I cleaned. I wiped up the coffee table, washed the dishes, and straightened up the apartment. An attempt to bring some order to my disorderly life. When I was done I still felt depressed and defeated, but at least things were tidy.

Later, when I went to Gina's room to say goodnight, I heard her talking on the phone. Pressing my ear against the door, I heard her say, "Don't cry, Allison, it'll be okay." I listened to her reassurances for the next ten minutes, and then I got really tired and went to bed.

Chapter 27

Rebel With a Cause

My mother and I didn't talk about moving for the rest of the week, but I made a decision of my own in the meantime. I wasn't going. I just wouldn't go. I could live with Kylie or Mason or in Nick's barn or foster care, under a bridge, whatever. I didn't care, as long as I could stay. I was physically Gina's match, maybe even bigger. There was no way she could force me to go.

All those years I didn't have a choice. Sometimes we left in the middle of the night, Gina carrying me out to the car half-asleep and me not waking up until we were two states away. That was my life then, because it was her life, but now I didn't want it anymore.

I'd taken a good look at my mother and saw what was really there. I wasn't sure what I wanted to do with my future, but she gave me a pretty clear picture of what I *didn't* want. I'd never put any child of mine through this. Things would be different in my world, once I had a say in things.

Along with my decision, there was another change in my life: Nick and I became a couple just like that. Two months ago we were strangers, and now, like connecting puzzle pieces, we were a perfect fit. Before I met him I didn't know it was possible to feel this way. Now I lived for the feel of his fingers intertwined with mine, and the way he looked at me like he couldn't believe his luck. He joked around a lot, which I loved. When we weren't together he called to say he was thinking of me and he couldn't wait until he saw me again. Gina's news was a dark cloud following me around that week, and he was the star that lit up my sky, the feeling that things would turn out okay despite the fact that I had the flakiest mother on the planet.

Kylie and Mason kidded me about my new boyfriend, but they approved and were happy for us. Even Allison was warmer—smiling when she saw me, talking about our classes with the ease of a friend. She told me she'd be lost without me and my mom, that no one else had been there for her in her darkest hour. She told me that I was lucky to have Gina as a mom, that no one else understood her at all. In the past I would have thought her talk was a little melodramatic, but now I mentally cut her a break. It wasn't easy starting over at a new school, not to mention losing your family and your home.

The news that Nick and I were together spread through the school. I think most everyone knew by Tuesday afternoon. Kylie overheard some of Crystal's friends talking in the bathroom. Apparently Crystal wasn't too shocked that Nick and I were together. He'd talked about me even while they were together—he thought I was interesting, smart, funny. The girls, of course, mocked me the whole time, but both Kylie and I thought this was good news. They could say I was taking Crystal's castoffs, but I didn't care.

At the end of the week Nick and I made plans to meet up with the others at the football game on Friday night. Lying on my bed Thursday evening with the phone against my ear, we talked about the weekend. Nick mentioned a movie we could see, if I wanted. Maybe going out to eat? "Or we could do both," he said.

On Saturday he'd have chores to do at home: apple picking and delivering some bushels to the local food pantry. "I can get it all done in the morning before I pick you up, or you can come along and help. Whatever you want, we'll do."

"I'll help you with the apples." There was no problem there. Apple picking was becoming one of my favorite things, and besides, Gina would be gone all day and into the night. "But I had something else in mind for later in the day, if you're up for it."

Chapter 28

Saturday Road Trip

Even though we were early they were ready for us, opening the door before we even knocked. After a flurry of introductions, there were hugs (for me) and handshaking (for Nick). When we got past the preliminaries, I noticed it was just Grandma and Grandpa. "Where's Aunt Dorothy and Uncle Bill?" I asked.

Grandma looked at Grandpa, then waved a hand in the air. "They had some errands to run, and we were feeling selfish and wanted you to ourselves."

I had mixed feelings about bringing Nick to meet my grandparents. It was pretty early in the relationship to start dragging him out and introducing him to the relatives, but the truth of it was, I needed the ride. I wanted to talk to them in person, and I didn't have any other way to get to Madison. I told myself it wasn't like I was using Nick. After all he *did* offer to take me anywhere I wanted to go. And I knew Grandma and Grandpa would enjoy meeting him. That was my rationale, anyway.

I gave Nick a tour of the house, all the while thinking about how important this visit was. In English class we'd discussed how an incident in a book became a "defining moment," which was another way of saying it was a turning point. I was ready for something like that in my life.

When we got to my room, I was glad to see that, as always, everything was exactly the way I left it. Vacuum marks on the carpeting showed that Grandma had cleaned, but otherwise nothing had changed. The stuffed animals I'd collected over the years sat on the ledge of the bay window, the bulletin board was covered with photos and ticket stubs. It was the one place in the world I could leave things and expect them to stay that way.

When we got back to the kitchen, Grandma was stirring soup on the stove and Grandpa was cutting a loaf of homemade bread. "I hope you kids haven't had lunch yet," he said, shaking the knife in my direction. "Your grandmother made enough for a whole Boy Scout troop."

"I'm really hungry," Nick said. "Everything smells wonderful."

Ten minutes later we were sitting around the kitchen table eating the best homemade chicken noodle soup ever.

"So where does your mother think you are today?" Grandma asked.

I dipped a chunk of bread into my bowl. "I told her I was spending the day with Nick and she could reach me on my cell phone anytime."

Grandpa chuckled. "Technically the truth, eh, Rae?"

"My mother knows we're here," Nick said. "Rae was at our place this morning helping me with my chores. My family owns an orchard."

"We brought you a bushel of apples," I said. "It's out in the truck. We'll bring it in before we leave."

Grandma smiled. "Then you'll have to come back next week for apple pie."

Nick said, "I'll come back every week if it means I'll get food this good."

Oh, he was smooth, but in a good way, and from the look on Grandma's face I saw she knew it too. The conversation was easy after that. Nick talked about his family, things I already knew about his older brother and sister and some Dunstan family history I hadn't heard before.

Grandpa told a few jokes, and Nick told a few back. I sat back and thought, *This must be what it feels like to be part of a family.* A functional, loving, stable family.

After lunch we all drifted in to the living room, where the fireplace was lit. On the other side of the room were the patio doors where you could watch birds at the feeders. Nick and I sat side by side on the loveseat; my grandparents sat in the wing chairs on either side of the fireplace. We were full from the soup and the homemade brownies my grandmother had served for dessert.

"So, Rae," Grandpa said, leaning forward. "When you called you said you had something to discuss with us?"

The room was quiet, all eyes on me. Nick had a curious look on his face. I hadn't told him about Gina's decision or what I wanted to ask my grandparents.

I had a whole speech planned, but when it came right down to it, I couldn't recall a word of it. I hadn't counted on being so nervous. Finally I just blurted out what I wanted. "Can I come and live with you?" They didn't have a chance to answer because suddenly words came out of me. A waterfall of words. I couldn't seem to stop. I told them about my mother hating her boss and wanting to move again at the end of the semester. I told them about my plan, which was that as soon as I turned sixteen I could get a job and a license and a car, live at their house and commute to Whitman High School every day. "If the weather is bad, I can stay overnight at my friend Kylie's house." I hadn't actually asked Kylie this, since she didn't know anything about it, but I couldn't imagine her saying no. "I don't need much, and I'll find a way to cover my gas and clothes and stuff." I'd thought through every objection they might have and tried to find an end around. I had $540 in hidden cash—money Grandma and Grandpa had given me over the years. It wouldn't buy a great car, but I'd looked on craigslist and occasionally there were cars for a few hundred dollars.

Nick didn't say anything during my outburst, but his mouth was set in a serious way and I felt his hand on the small of my back.

"Rae, darling girl," Grandma said when I was done. "We would love nothing better than to have you live with us, believe me, but I don't think your mother would ever allow it."

Grandpa made a funny noise in his throat and got up to stir the fire with a poker. His shoulders slumped, and I saw him lift a hand to his face.

Grandma continued. "We've offered in the past to have you or both of you come and live with us, for however long she wanted. Gina would have none of it."

Grandpa returned the poker to its stand. "It made her mad. One year she was having such money troubles we pressed the issue, and she got so angry she refused to come at Christmas."

I remembered that year. I was seven and my mother had told me Grandma and Grandpa had other plans for the holidays. That it would be more fun to go out to eat and to a movie with her then boyfriend. I think his name was Owen, but maybe Owen came later.

"So I don't have a choice in the matter—I just have to keep moving?" I blinked back tears. I'd been so sure they would help me. "Because you know it won't end. We never stay anywhere."

"I'm so sorry, Rae." Grandma was near tears, I could tell. "Grandpa and I even looked into getting legal custody of you, but your mother didn't fit the criteria of an unfit mother. You weren't abused or neglected. You always went to school and got good grades. We had no legal grounds."

"Living like a nomad isn't illegal," Grandpa said. "And you never complained, just rose to the occasion. We always marveled at how well adjusted you were." He sat on the ottoman in front of me and looked straight at me, his eyes filled with regret. "If we could do it, we would in a heartbeat, you have to know that, Rae."

"I know," I said. I knew if it were up to them I could show up at their door anytime and they'd take me in. Unfortunately, it wasn't up to them.

"Maybe if it comes from you, she might be more open," Grandma said. "You can ask her, but don't say you've spoken to us about it, or she'll shoot the idea down for sure."

I nodded. Nick rubbed my lower back with small, comforting strokes. I wiped my eyes. "But if she says yes, you're okay with it? I can come and live with you?"

"Oh Rae," Grandma said sadly, "of course it would be okay with us. But don't get your hopes up. I know my own daughter. She's never given an inch before, and I doubt she's going to start now."

Chapter 29

Change of View

"Why didn't you tell me you were moving?" Nick asked, backing out of the driveway. When he glanced my way I couldn't meet his eyes. Looking down at my lap, it was hard to see through the tears welling in my eyes. I didn't want to tell him the real reason I hadn't said anything—that I was afraid he wouldn't want to bother with a girl who was going to be gone by Christmastime. I'd seen it happen time and time again. As soon as my "friends" heard I was moving, they started distancing themselves. I saw them scouting out my replacement before I'd even packed a box. It hurt. And this time it would hurt even more because it wasn't just a friend, it was Nick.

"I guess," I said finally, a few blocks later, "I was hoping to figure out a way not to move. I thought for sure—" I had to stop for a gulp of air. "I thought that my grandparents would take me in. I was so sure of it."

At my grandparents' house reality had hit me smack in the face. I could see now that my plans of living under a bridge or staying at a friend's would never work. Gina's need for change would win again, and I'd be dragged along with her. It was all too much to think about.

You know when you try to hold back crying, and then it builds and builds and finally explodes in one ugly-sounding sob? That's exactly what happened then. This big phlegm-in-my-throat noise came out of nowhere, and I started crying. I put my head in my hands, wishing I'd thought to bring Kleenex. I said, "I'm sorry," but it came out all garbled. I was sure Nick would think I was a complete emo psycho. I pictured him on Monday going back to Blake's table in the lunchroom and reuniting with Crystal, who had to realize by now that Trey Griffin had nothing on Nick. "I'm so sorry."

Nick pulled the truck over to the side of the road and put it into park, then slid closer and wrapped his arms around me. He made these shh-ing noises over and over again; it was almost hypnotic. I felt my breathing start to relax. "It's okay, it's okay," he murmured. "We'll figure something out."

I wiped my eyes with the back of my hand. My eyeliner was in danger of major smudging. "There's really nothing to figure out," I said sadly. "We're moving and that's it. My mom always acts like I have some say in the matter, but I don't. She just rents a trailer, packs up the car, and we go. End of story."

He kissed the top of my head. "Do you think it would help if my mom talks to her? Explains how important it is to finish high school in one place? Maybe if your mom thinks of it in terms of how it will affect you getting into college, she'll reconsider."

His voice was reassuring, but I could tell he didn't get it. When Gina wanted to go, she was like a tornado at ground level. Nothing stood in her way. "I already told her that, but it didn't help," I said sadly. "There's no reasoning with her when she gets this way."

We were quiet for a few minutes, me sitting miserably while Nick stroked my head. I wanted to blot out the rest of the world and make it so it was just us: two people in a Ford truck, the heater humming quietly and the cardboard air freshener dangling from the rearview mirror.

"It's not like you'll be dropping off the planet," he said, breaking the silence. "We can phone and text and Skype. And we can visit back and forth. Next year I'll be eighteen, and I'll drive to wherever you are."

Next year? That was forever to me. A person could pack a lifetime of memories into twelve months. I'd miss prom, Valentine's Day, opening day at the ballpark, senior skip day, summer days at the lake. Somewhere in there Nick would find someone else, and those would become her memories. Then he'd be off to college and a whole new group of friends. Eventually we'd wind up leaving messages for each other on Facebook, and when his new, prettier girlfriend asked who I was he'd say, "Just this girl I went out with in high school for like a month." That's who I would become—some girl he once knew.

"Really, Rae," he said, lifting my chin with his finger, "we'll stay in touch, I promise. I don't want to lose you."

His lips against mine were the best cure for my troubles. I held him and thought, *How could I possibly be apart from Nick?* It would just be cruel.

We made out madly, clinging to each other for I don't know how long, and we would have continued until time ended, the sun burned out, and the earth froze, except my phone, that damn phone, went off again.

He paused. "Are you going to get that?"

"No." Nothing was that important. I ignored it, and it stopped after a minute. "See, all gone." I smiled and put my hands on either side of his beautiful head. We'd barely reconnected when whoever was calling tried again.

"What if it's your grandparents?" Nick asked.

Sighing, I reached down to pull the phone out of my bag. I flipped it open. "I don't know this number." The moment was ruined anyway. Might as well answer it.

"Hello?"

"Rae?" It was Gina. "This is an emergency. Allison's missing. I'm calling from her aunt's house. How soon can you get here?"

Chapter 30

Big Problem, Hot Cop

"What do you mean Allison's missing?" I asked, switching to speakerphone so Nick could hear it too.

"She's missing. I don't know how else to put it." Gina sounded kind of pissed off at my question, which was so unfair. It wasn't my fault. "Do you have any idea where she could be?"

"No." I looked at Nick, who shrugged.

"She sent this long e-mail to you, Kylie, and Mason saying she was just in the way and that she was running away. Her aunt hasn't seen her since last night. She assumed she was in her room all this time. Can you come right away? A police officer is coming to the house and has some questions for you."

"We just delivered a bushel of apples to this old couple's house." I tried not to look at Nick, who looked amused at how I'd sidestepped the truth. "We're probably forty-five minutes away, but we'll get there as fast as we can."

Nick pulled away from the curb as I finished up the conversation. My mother warned us not to drive too fast, but to get there as soon as possible. "I'm really worried about her," was one of the last things Gina said. "Her e-mail sounds almost suicidal."

I closed the phone, repeating that part to Nick. "Poor Allison. She must be at such a low point, I can't even imagine."

"Yeah, she got a raw deal, no doubt about it."

We didn't say much more on the drive back. Nick fiddled with the radio stations, and I listened to my voice mail: three messages from Kylie telling me about Allison's e-mail. She must have called while my bag was in my grandparents' front hall closet.

When we pulled into Blake's driveway a squad car was already there, parked behind my mother's Saturn. Mrs. Daly met us at the door and ushered us into the living room, where my mother sat opposite a young cop in full uniform. He was jotting down notes when we walked in, but stood up when we entered.

"Thank God you're here," my mother said, rushing over to hug me. You'd have thought I was the one gone missing.

The extremely good-looking police officer, Officer Brent, gave us the rundown. The e-mail had been sent in the middle of the night, making them think Allison left around three in the morning.

"I didn't hear anything, honest," Mrs. Daly said, as if someone had suggested otherwise. "I had no idea she even knew how to disable the alarm system." I'd envisioned Blake's mom to be this uncaring, society diva, but this woman, wearing a plain velour running suit, looked sick with worry.

Kylie had gone to see Mrs. Daly as soon as she read the e-mail, around noon, and the police had interviewed Kylie and Blake's family before we got there. We just missed Kylie, who had to leave to attend a family reunion. No one had been able to reach Mason, who was participating in a mathematics competition in Green Bay for the day.

Mrs. Daly told me that Blake and his father were driving around looking for Allison. "Dan is sick about this," she said.

I assumed Dan was her husband. "It was hard enough losing his brother and Tammy, but if anything happens to Allison..." She dabbed her eyes with a tissue.

"They will find her," my mother said firmly, then handed me a printout of the e-mail.

I swallowed hard and read every heartbreaking word. The first sentence said, "Thank you for your friendship, not that I deserve it." After that Allison went on to say she was always letting people down. That she couldn't stand herself or her life anymore and couldn't live with the nightmares she had every night. She said it was like reliving the night of the fire over and over again. Blake hated her—that came up several times in the e-mail—and she knew he didn't want her living there, so she was leaving and never coming back. "Don't tell anyone," she wrote. "I don't want them looking for me."

So much for that.

Officer Brent asked Nick and me questions. Did we have any idea where Allison might go? Did she have a boyfriend or other friends besides us? Would someone have lent her a car or driven her to the bus station? Did she have money, that we knew of?

I was a pretty worthless informant, and Nick knew less than me. When the police officer was done questioning us and taking down our full names and contact information, he assured Mrs. Daly that they would have an alert put out for Allison. "If she's on foot, she didn't go far. A lot of times teenagers who are upset are found at friends' houses. We find they often cool off and come back on their own in less than twenty-four hours." He slid his pen into the spiral of his notebook, handed each of us his card, and said he'd be in touch.

While Mrs. Daly showed him to the door, Gina whispered, "Did you get a look at that cop? He's hot." She craned her neck to get one last look at his backend.

"Hopefully he's good at finding people too," I said. "Because in case you forgot, Allison's missing."

"I know that." She frowned and shook her head. "I can't believe Allison didn't think to call me if she was that unhappy. I would have helped her. She could have lived with us, even."

"Except that we're moving." I couldn't hide the bitterness in my voice. How was it that she was all over helping Allison and yet didn't give a damn about her own daughter?

"Well, there's no way we'd move if Allison was going to live with us," she said, my tone lost on her, apparently. "Because she'd need stability after everything she's gone through."

"Allison would need stability? You have got to be kidding. What about me?" I gave her a WTF look. Her attitude was infuriating. "Lady, you are unbelievable." I got out of my chair and stood over her.

"What's your problem, Rae?" She stood up too, and now we were eye to eye. Blake's mother came back and opened her mouth to speak, then closed it when she saw us facing off.

"My problem is you. I can't believe you'd put off moving for Allison, when you wouldn't do it for me, your own daughter."

Gina looked up at me, thick lashes framing big eyes. She was puzzled, was how it looked. How could she not know why this angered me? "Maybe this is a conversation we should have later on."

"It's always later on with you," I said. Nick got up to put a steadying hand on my shoulder.

Mrs. Daly cleared her throat, which broke the tension. Wringing her hands, she said, "Would anyone like something to drink?"

"No thank you," Nick said. "I think we should probably get going."

"Okay then." Relief showed in Mrs. Daly's face. "Thank you for all your help. I can't even tell you how much I appreciate it."

My mother got up and gave Mrs. Daly a hug. "Make sure you call as soon as you hear something, Meg."

"I will." Mrs. Daly looked at Nick and me. "I feel just terrible about this. The psychiatrist said Allison was making such progress, and she seemed so much happier to me. She finally let me buy her some new clothes. We went shopping together and had such a good time. I just can't believe she just up and left. I told her over and over again to ignore Blake. He's used to being an only child, but I knew he'd adjust eventually."

"We'll get her back," Gina said. "It'll work out."

Mrs. Daly didn't look so sure. "I hope so."

Chapter 31

Tell Me What You Really Think

We drove behind my mother's car all the way back to my apartment. "Did you want me to drop you off so you and your mother can talk?" Nick asked.

"Are you kidding? I need you there or else I'll kill her."

He chuckled deep in his throat, a real guy laugh. To me, his laughter was the exact sound of happiness. That and the feel of his arms was all I needed to survive.

"It's not that funny. I really want to kill her."

"I know. That's what makes it funny."

We parked in the front and gave my mom some lead time so that when we walked in together, she'd already be there. And she was, there I mean, hands on her hips, which I knew meant trouble. I'd seen that position when she was telling off boyfriends, sniping at my grandmother, practicing "I quit" speeches for the employers she'd grown sick of.

"Hi, Mom," I said, all cheerful-like, so that I would seem like the calm, reasonable one.

"Don't even start with that." Did she realize how bitchy she sounded? I resisted the urge to look at Nick. She took a step closer to me. "What the hell was your problem back there?"

"What, I'm not entitled to speak my mind?"

"I hardly thought it was appropriate to start a fight with me when Allison is missing. Can you imagine what poor Mrs. Daly is going through? She didn't need to hear you making a big stink about something that hasn't even happened yet."

This was a whole new experience for me—we disagreed on occasion, but I never let it get heated. I spent my whole life having the cool mom, and I loved her, I really did, despite her crazy ways. In general I always went along with whatever she wanted, and if she got the least bit angry I always backed off.

Maybe it was because Nick was standing next to me, or maybe because we were the same size, but suddenly I didn't care anymore if she was pissed off. Let her be mad—I was mad too, so we were equal.

"Okay," I said, "I probably shouldn't have said anything in front of Mrs. Daly, but I just lost it. How is it that we're going to move again, even though I don't want to, but for Allison you'd stay? You care more about some girl you just met than your own daughter? How is that supposed to make me feel?"

"Now you're talking stupid and being selfish, Rae. This conversation is over." She turned around and stalked off to the kitchen.

I followed, speaking to her back. "No, I'm not being selfish. I'm just telling you the way it is with me. What, I can't say how I feel? If anything, that makes you the selfish one."

She picked up a pack of cigarettes off the table and rapped at the end until one slid out. "Comparing yourself to Allison is hardly fair. Allison is going through emotional hell. You are fine.

You are always fine, and I resent the implication that our moving so much is somehow screwing up your life. You make friends easily, you do well in school—if anything, you should thank me. I stayed in one spot my whole childhood, and it was no walk in the park, believe me. It was the most joyless existence you can imagine. Everything the same, always the same. You, on the other hand, have lived everywhere, seen everything." She snapped open her lighter and put a Marlboro between her lips. "I would have killed for that opportunity." Putting the flame to the end of the cigarette, she inhaled until the tip glowed.

"I have seen *nothing*." I had to fight to keep control of my voice. "You think it's different, but it's all the same—the same crappy apartments, the same being new all the time. I never fit in anywhere, thanks to you."

We stood there for a moment, not saying anything. I could sense Nick behind me in the doorway. Finally my mom said, "Well, you are welcome, Rae. We always had so much fun together, I guess I somehow missed the part where I completely screwed up your life."

I felt the tears start up again. I hated crying. I couldn't believe I was doing it twice in one day. "I don't want to fight with you. We did have fun sometimes. I don't know why we can't just stay put for once. Just this one time, until I'm done with high school."

She reached down and set her cigarette on the edge of the ashtray. "You never said much about moving before. I thought I was giving you the world."

"I didn't want the world." Blinking back tears, I said, "I just wanted to be home." I said the words and something clicked in my head, like the mechanism in a combination lock: *clink*. It echoed in my brain. *Just wanted to be home.*

And that's when I knew where Allison went.

Chapter 32

Again, A Road Trip

Home. The word comes up time and time again. Home cooking. Hometown hero. Home sweet home.

Soldiers stationed overseas dream of home. Dorothy went all the way to Oz to learn there's no place like home. In baseball, every batter tries to make it home with one powerful hit. A home run.

Where was Allison? My best guess was home, even if home wasn't there anymore.

Originally we were all going to go, but Gina worried that Allison might show up at our apartment and feel abandoned if no one was there. I suggested it be just Nick and me, but Gina worried about two high school students making a car trip two hours each way. Finally Nick, greatest guy in the world, offered to wait at our apartment in case Allison showed up. Not that I thought that would happen. I was sure she was long gone, but Gina wasn't as convinced. I would rather have driven with Nick than my mom, but this was the only solution that satisfied her.

"Are you sure we take I-94 west?" my mother asked as she turned onto the expressway.

"I got the directions from Google maps and MapQuest. What are the chances they'd be the same *and* both be wrong?" I'd gotten the address from the newspaper article about the fire at Allison's house. It had her house number on Magnolia Drive and the name of a neighbor. It was a start.

Gina pursed her lips and reached for the Mountain Dew in the cup holder. We'd stopped for gas on the way out of town and stocked up on road trip snacks. She took a sip and set it back without taking her eyes off the road. "I hope you're right about this. It's a long way to go if she's not there."

"But wouldn't it be sad if she was there and we never looked?"

My mother sighed. "I want to find her, Rae, as much as anyone else. It just seems so far for someone without a car. And Meg said the police in that community have been notified and are on the lookout for her." This was Blake's mother. Apparently we were all friends now.

"She would avoid them," I said. "But if she saw us, she'd come out from wherever she is. I know she would." At least I hoped so.

"I just have so much trouble understanding why Allison's stories don't add up," Mom said, her fingertips tapping the steering wheel. "Meg told me that they *wanted* Allison to come live with them. A group of relatives got together and decided Meg and her husband were the best choice because they had the big house and the financial resources to help her. Did you know that the Dalys are all going to family counseling to help Allison adjust? Meg said it was helping all of them."

"Yeah, Blake said something about family counseling. He was pretty pissed about it."

"So it's true then." She took another sip of soda. At this rate we'd have to make a potty stop before we even got there. "Another thing Allison told me was that her aunt couldn't be bothered

157

taking her shopping for clothes and school supplies, but Meg said she begged her to go to the mall with her, and Allison said she didn't want new things, she preferred to wear Meg's clothes."

"Hmmm."

"I mean, Allison said these things right to my face, and they were out-and-out lies. Why would she do that?"

"Because she's a messed-up kid?"

"Yeah, but that messed up?"

I shrugged. "Maybe from her point of view it wasn't a lie. Maybe that's how she really saw it."

"But it was the complete opposite of how it really was."

"Well, look at you and Grandma and Grandpa. They said they were trying to help you when you were a teenager. You thought they were trying to ruin your life."

She opened her mouth and then seemed to think better of it, her lips coming together in one thin line. "Mmmm." I think I made my point.

The rest of the trip was spent with me reading directions and Gina restlessly changing radio stations. Every time I got into a good song, she switched to something else. Finally I swatted her hand away. "You drive, I'll be in charge of the music."

Just outside of Allison's hometown we stopped at a QuikTrip, me to double-check directions, Mom to make a bathroom stop. There were two guys behind the counter watching some sports show on a small TV. When I walked up, the younger one leaned over the counter and smiled. I showed him the address, and he confirmed that we were headed in the right direction. Then I handed him Allison's photo from the newspaper article. "Have you seen this girl recently?" I asked.

He took the paper from my hand and showed it to his co-worker, an older guy with a gray beard, before answering my question. "Allison Daly? She went to school with my little brother, but I haven't seen her since the funeral. You a friend of hers?"

I explained that I knew her from her new high school and that she was missing. "If you see her, notify the police immediately," I said.

"She won't be coming around here," he said with a laugh. "Not after what she did. What kind of psycho burns down their own house?" He handed the paper back to me. "Even her own boyfriend wouldn't talk to her after that."

"I heard it was an accident."

He shrugged and said, "They never proved it, but everyone knows she started that fire on purpose. She and her folks were at war. Her mom grounded her and took away her cell phone, and Allison was mad as hell. She told everyone at the high school she was going to get her parents. She was going to make them sorry." He nudged the other guy. "I guess she did make them sorry, hey?"

The other guy nodded. "Bill Clark, my cousin, was working the firehouse that night, and he was the one who found her. She was drunk as a skunk, he said, and talking all kinds of stupidity. Said she fell asleep outside, like anyone would believe that."

I felt a chill go up my back. Even when Allison was being cold toward me, I never would have believed she'd deliberately set a house on fire with her parents inside. I mutely stepped away from the counter, letting a man in overalls pay for his gas. When my mom came out of the bathroom, I met her at the door.

As we headed out, she said, "Are our directions okay?"

I nodded. "Yeah, we're right on track."

Chapter 33

You Can Never Go Home Again

Allison's hometown was one of those places you see on Christmas cards. The center of town had a park with a bandstand, perfect for concerts on summer nights. A small café sat next to Joe's Barbershop. Across the street was a Piggly Wiggly and a hardware store. We passed a fire and police station, both in the same building. The same guy probably ran both, that's the kind of quiet small town it was.

I gave Mom directions down a country road, where the houses were further apart.

We had to zig and zag and turn again to reach Magnolia Drive. When we reached the crossroads, my mother stopped the car and we both looked up at the sign. "Are you ready for this?" She reached over and squeezed my arm.

"I think so."

She turned left while I checked the address. "We're looking for 612." We both scanned the mailboxes, checking the numbers. As we counted down, she eased off the accelerator and the car slowed to a crawl.

Both of us spotted it at the same time. We could have been doing fifty-five and we'd still have seen it. A lone lamppost in the front yard illuminated the ruins. We pulled into the driveway and stopped alongside the light. "Oh my God," Gina said.

We got out of the car and walked to where the house had been. Now it was an open basement filled with junk: burned wood and shingles. Stakes had been pounded in the ground at each corner, and yellow caution tape linked them. The trees closest to the house looked charred and dead.

We stood where the front porch must have been and looked down. It was hard to believe this foundation once held a house— walls and furniture, a roof. Without speaking we slowly circled the perimeter. Bulldozer tracks came right up to the edge of the basement walls. In back was a concrete slab, filthy with dirt and soot. I guessed it was once a patio, the place where the newspaper article said Allison's dad loved to have cookouts with friends. I tried to imagine a group of people there, laughing and talking as burgers sizzled on the grill, but it was impossible for me to get a visual.

"This is even worse than I pictured," Gina said, which was exactly what I was thinking. There was nothing here but wreckage. Nothing for Allison to come back to. I knew the house had burned down, but somehow I'd pictured the property with some other structure—a shed maybe, or a garage. I imagined we'd find her huddled inside, just waiting to be found. That we'd talk her into coming back. Save her. It sounds delusional, I know, like I thought we'd be heroes or something, but it wasn't just about me. I honestly had a strong feeling she'd go back home, pulled to the place she belonged for sixteen years.

"Now what?" Gina asked. "Should we drive back into town and ask around? She might have gone to a friend's. Best-case scenario she's in someone's house right now playing Guitar Hero and thinking about calling her aunt." Somewhere in the last few hours my mom had gotten less concerned, and I'd gotten more.

I thought of what the QuikTrip guys had said, how Allison's boyfriend wouldn't even talk to her anymore. They made her sound like a social pariah. I somehow doubted she'd reconnect with old friends. "She never mentioned any friends here. I got the impression she's sort of distanced herself from everyone in her past."

"Should we check with the neighbors and see if they've seen anything?" She looked at me expectantly. My mom was all about action, while I liked to think things through.

"I guess." But I didn't move. I just wanted a little more time here. It was unrealistic, I knew, but I still hoped to find some clue that would lead us to Allison. "Maybe you could go and I'll wait with the car? Just in case?"

Gina nodded and pointed off to our right. "I'll try there first."

After she'd left I walked around the house again. I tried to imagine Allison getting off the school bus and walking up the gravel drive to the house. Was her mother there to greet her, to ask about her day? I tried to remember if the newspaper article said something about her parents' jobs, but all I could recall was that Tammy Daly led the local Girl Scout troop. What a sad legacy—she left behind one screwed-up daughter, a burned-down house, and a group of girls who'd remember her for organizing the cookie drive and doing whatever else Girl Scout leaders did. I never got a chance to join, so I was a little foggy on the details.

It was dusk now, getting dark and colder too. I went to the car and got the flashlight out of the glove compartment. I pushed the button, happy when a bright beam of light snapped on. Off in the distance I could see my mom standing on the neighbor's front porch, gesturing as she talked to someone in the house.

I circled around the caution tape, swinging the light toward the ground. Something rustled in the woods behind the house, freaking me out a little. I froze for a minute, and then relaxed when I saw a bird fly out and pass overhead.

"Allison?" I called out. "Allison, can you hear me?" I didn't really think she was within earshot, but I had to try. I walked closer to the trees and said her name over and over again, my own personal mantra. I said it so many times that it started to feel like a foreign language: Al-li-son. In my head I heard her say my name in return.

I stopped and called out her name again. "Allison?" I heard my name again, but this time it came from outside of me, in the direction of the thicket of trees. I held my breath. Was it the wind? No.

"Rae."

My heart quickened. Out of the corner of my eye I saw my mother and a strange man walking on the road toward me. Some kind of electric lantern dangled from the man's hand.

"Rae." Now I knew I heard it.

It was her. I walked toward the voice, past the tree line, into woods so thick I wouldn't have been able to see at all if not for the flashlight. "Allison, where are you?"

"Here. I'm here." I barely heard her voice, and yet it was enough to guide me.

When I found her she was sitting with her back against a tree, a backpack at her side. On the ground next to her, a hunting knife and a container of pills rested on top of a piece of folded lined paper. The beam from my flashlight showed dirt smears on her face and blotchy bloodstains on the edges of her white sweatshirt sleeves. Her hair stuck up in clumps. The relief on her face when she recognized me broke my heart. All I could think was what if we hadn't come? I knelt down and smoothed the hair away from her face. "It's okay, everything's going to be okay."

She clutched at my sleeve and pulled me close. "Help me, Rae."

Chapter 34

First to Aid, Last to Leave

The man walking with my mother turned out to be Jim Benson, the same neighbor who'd called 911 the night of the fire. I'm not sure if it was a good omen or a bad sign that he was involved again, but he made the call this time too. After he was done explaining the situation to the operator, he walked out to the driveway to wait for the ambulance.

Gina stayed with me, but she wasn't much help. As soon as she saw the blood she started freaking out, hyperventilating and making suggestions about CPR, which wasn't appropriate at all since Allison was clearly breathing and had a heartbeat. While she was talking nonsense about compressions, my health class first aid training kicked in. The cuts on Allison's wrists didn't seem to be bleeding anymore, but she might have been in shock, so I had my mom help shift her position until she was lying flat. Then we elevated her feet using the backpack and covered her with a blanket we kept in the trunk.

When Gina left to see if we had a water bottle in the car, Allison said, "I'm sorry, Rae."

"It's okay, Allison. Don't worry about it. You've been through a lot. Help is on the way." I pulled the blanket up to her chin.

She pulled my hair so my ear was level with her lips. "I never told you my secret that night," she whispered, "but I'm ready to tell now."

"It's okay, you don't have to, really."

"No, I want to." It was hard for her to speak, I could tell. She was talking softly, with long pauses between each word. "My secret is that the fire *was* my fault. But I didn't burn my house down on purpose, I swear. I forgot about the candle."

I pulled back and looked right in her eyes. "I know, Allison, it's okay."

"The candle was for my boyfriend Zach. It was our sign. I put it on the porch so he would know to meet me in the woods. Zach and I fell asleep out here, and when I woke up the house was on fire. I didn't want my mom and dad to die. You have to believe me."

"I believe you."

She closed her eyes, and for a few minutes we were alone in the world. I arranged the blanket snugly around her—she was shivering now—and smoothed her hair away from her face. Then the stillness was broken by the sound of a siren as the ambulance approached. Soon I could see the flash of light through the trees and hear the sound of men's voices and the crunch of boots on gravel.

My mom's voice said, "This way."

Within moments three men came into the clearing, one carrying what looked like a large tackle box, the others carrying a stretcher on wheels. I stepped aside and they went into emergency mode, checking Allison's vitals, assessing her injuries, and eventually moving her from the ground onto the gurney. My mom,

Jim Benson, and I stood on the sidelines. A few minutes earlier I'd made all the difference. Now I was in the way.

The rest of it went by in a blur. After the ambulance drove away with Allison, the police arrived to question us and take down our information. From there we drove to the local hospital and called Blake's mom, then Nick, Kylie, and Mason.

The phone call to Mason was the most awkward. His team had placed first in the statewide mathematics competition, so it was one of those good news/bad news phone conversations with me saying congratulations and him feeling terrible that he wasn't there during the crisis. That's how life is, I guess. While some people are attempting to die, other people are rejoicing because they really know their trigonometry.

We sat waiting for news about Allison, but no one would tell us anything because we weren't relatives. I shifted in my seat, but couldn't get comfortable. Above us a buzzing florescent light cast a harsh light.

Mom fidgeted with her fingers. I thought she was going to excuse herself and go outside for a smoke. Instead she said, "I once tried to kill myself, you know."

I sat up straight. "When was this?"

"In high school. I took a butt-load of sleeping pills. I was staying overnight at my friend Vickie's house. I stole the pills out of her mom's medicine cabinet."

There was a long pause while I waited for her to tell me more. I knew the end of the story—obviously Gina lived—but I wanted to know what came after the pills and before she became my mother. "Why did you want to die?"

"Typical story. I was depressed. I had boyfriend trouble, a lot of stress in my life. It all seemed like too much."

"Why didn't you talk to your parents if you had problems?"

She snorted. "They were the cause of most of my problems. It wasn't easy being their daughter, trust me. They had high expectations. I couldn't get a break. Nothing I did was ever good enough. They were always on me about my grades. They hated my friends, my makeup, the way I dressed. When I turned eighteen, I couldn't get away fast enough. I would have stayed away forever except for you. You were so beautiful. I wanted to show them I finally did something right."

"Grandma said they didn't even know I existed until I was a toddler."

"Yeah, and you know what she said when they first met you?"

I looked at her expectantly.

"I told them your name, and she said, 'Oh Gina, no, please tell me you're kidding. You didn't really name her Rae, did you?'"

She didn't like my name? I loved my name. It was different, but not too weird. "What's wrong with Rae?"

Mom shrugged. "I told you, nothing I do is good enough for them."

"They're not like that anymore, though," I said, defending them. "Grandma only says good things about you now."

"I bet."

Man, Gina could hold a grudge. "So what happened after you took the sleeping pills?"

She sighed. "It was kind of an impulsive thing. I wasn't going to tell anyone, but when I felt the pills starting to take effect I told Vickie. She freaked out and called my parents, and they had me rushed to the hospital. After that, they shipped me off to a mental institution for a month. When I went back to school, I was this freak, this wacko head case. Guess what? No one wants to take the suicidal girl to prom."

"Hey, wait a minute," I said, tapping her arm. "You told me Grandma and Grandpa sent you to the mental hospital for no reason at all. You told me that they lied about you being suicidal. Why did you say that?"

"I was still pissed off about it. And you know what?" she said. "I wasn't really suicidal, if you want to know the complete truth. Yes, I did take the pills, but I wasn't serious about killing myself. The emergency room doctor said the amount of drugs in my system wouldn't have killed me. I would have made it through the night, and the next day I would have felt better and the whole thing would have passed. I could have just continued with my life if they hadn't overreacted and sent me to the nut-job factory."

"But they didn't know all that. They thought they were losing their daughter. They were probably scared."

"I guess."

A woman in scrubs pushed a cart past our feet. One of the wheels spun crazily around like it had a mind of its own. I waited until the soft swoosh of her footsteps had receded down the hallway, and then I said, "What do you think Grandma and Grandpa should have done instead?"

"They could have talked to me, for starters. They never talked *to* me. Not once. They were always talking *at* me. They never even bothered to find out what I wanted out of life. It was all about them and what they wanted."

"But they want to talk to you now," I said softly. "They try all the time, but you never give them a chance." I leaned over and rested my head on her shoulder. Even now, at the end of a long day, I could still smell her berry-scented shampoo. "Couldn't you at least give them a chance and try to be nice to them? For me?" I looked up and gave her the puppy-dog eyes.

She lowered her head so we were almost nose to nose. "You're asking a lot of me, Rae."

"Please?"

She gave me a thin-lipped smile. "Okay, I'll see what I can do."

We sat there for a little bit longer, wondering all the while if we should just go home, but feeling like we should stay. Finally one of the nurses, a cute young one with short, dark hair, took pity on us. "You didn't hear it from me," she whispered conspiratorially, "but your friend is going to be fine. The wounds on her wrists weren't angled enough to cause a fatal blood loss, and she didn't take anywhere near enough pills for it to be lethal. She's sleeping peacefully now, and we have someone with her."

"Her aunt and uncle are on the way," my mom said.

The nurse nodded. "We're aware of this; we've talked to them."

There was nothing left to do then but get in the Saturn and drive home.

Chapter 35
Bad News Travels Like Wildfire

Everyone at school had heard about Allison's failed suicide attempt by Monday afternoon. Kids who looked right through me before now stopped me in the halls to ask about it. Suddenly I was worthy.

I didn't give up much—yes, I said, Allison ran away, yes, my mom and I found her at her old house. Yes, she was in the hospital now. Anything past that I pleaded ignorance. I believed Allison deserved her privacy even if Blake, the bigmouth, didn't agree. He told everyone about the e-mail she'd sent and that the police had interviewed all of us after she'd gone missing. I heard through the Whitman grapevine that she'd hitchhiked nearly all the way there in the middle of the night, and that she'd spent the weekend in the hospital but was being transferred as an inpatient back to our local Mental Health Unit for Children and Adolescents.

By lunchtime Tuesday, sick of hearing people ask about Blake's cousin, I was glad to be leaving early, right after lunch. This time it was no surprise. My mother had written a note excusing me from school so the two of us could visit Allison at MHUCA. The day before, Meg had called, saying Allison wanted to speak to both of us as soon as possible.

When we got there, my mom and I went through the same entrance I'd used with Blake. We got buzzed through the door and signed in at the front desk. The woman there directed us to a visiting room on the second floor. Three minutes later we sat on a vinyl-covered couch in a tiny room, glass walls all around.

Allison walked in right after we did. She wore her regular clothes and looked fine. The only things different about her were the white bandages peeking out from the edges of her sleeves. My mom got up from the couch right away and gave her a hug, and I did too—for some reason it seemed natural now. I guess when you've seen someone at their lowest point, there's nothing left to get in the way.

"How're you doing, hon?" my mom asked.

"Pretty good."

"You look *really* good," I said and regretted it as soon as I saw the look on her face. Unspoken were the words: *compared to the last time I saw you, when you were trying to kill yourself.* I tried to cover my blunder. "I'm glad you're better."

"Thanks." She smiled shyly.

After we sat down, Allison and me on the couch, my mom on a molded plastic chair just opposite us, Allison said, "I don't know if you've heard, but I've been kind of depressed lately." She made a kind of fake, throat-clearing laugh, to show she was joking.

"But you're better now, right?" Gina asked.

"Not really." She looked down at her hands. "I don't want to die anymore, but I don't really feel like living either."

My mom looked alarmed. "You don't mean that. A beautiful girl like you, Allison, you have so much to look forward to. I know you've been through a terrible ordeal, losing your parents and all, but you still have a lot to live for. You have your whole life ahead of you. Don't you agree, Rae?"

"I think," I said slowly, "that it's okay for Allison to feel like that. You can't always just brush away your problems and move on. Sometimes you have to work through things. Don't you agree, Mom?"

I could tell by the look on her face that my words hit home. She recovered pretty quickly though and turned to Allison, saying, "Of course you should take all the time you need to get through this, hon. You've been through a lot."

Allison nodded and twisted her hands. "I wanted to see you guys today to thank you for all you've done for me. Both of you have been great, really. And I also wanted to tell you myself that I'm not going back to Whitman. I can't live at Blake's house anymore, or deal with all the people at school knowing about me. It's just too much to deal with."

"So what will you be doing?" I asked.

"I'm going to stay here as an inpatient for a while. My doctor and I put together a plan. They have an alternative school right on the grounds, and I'll go there for now. It didn't really work out at Uncle Dan and Aunt Meg's, so when I'm better I'm probably going to live with my aunt and uncle in Iowa. They never had kids, and they say they want me."

"Iowa is really nice," my mom said. "We lived in Des Moines for a year. When was that, Rae?"

I shrugged. Who could keep track? "I don't remember Des Moines." I turned my attention to Allison. "So you're going to keep living here for now?" Through the glass wall I saw a woman in a business suit stride past, her high heels clicking on the linoleum.

Allison gestured in a circular motion. "This is it for the next few weeks. Right back where I started from. Remember when I first saw you, Rae, right outside in the yard?" She pointed toward the back of the building.

"I remember. You tried to warn me about the other kids, but I didn't understand. They scared the hell out of me when they rushed the fence."

Gina looked puzzled, but she didn't say anything. I knew I'd have some explaining to do later.

"You didn't *look* scared." Allison tucked a stray lock of hair behind her ear. "You just picked up your backpack and walked away like it was nothing. And then later when I got the tour of the school with Mr. Smedley I saw you in the lunchroom. I knew right away it was you."

"That was the day Blake slipped and fell down next to our table."

She nodded. "He was so pissed off, and you just laughed. Then when he was about to get in your face, Mason stepped up to protect you, like he was your bodyguard or something. I thought, *That has to be the coolest girl I've ever seen.*"

Me? No one ever thought I was cool before.

"I was such a mess. When I saw you, I could tell you weren't afraid of anything. That's why I asked Mr. Smedley to pair you up with me."

"But you weren't very friendly after that. I mean, considering you asked for me and everything."

"I know. I'm not sure why." She looked down at her lap. "Maybe because I was afraid you'd think I was this big loser and not want to hang out with me."

"I would never think that." I meant it, too.

"Oh, Allison." Gina got up to sit between us and wrapped her arms around her. She was good at comforting people. "You poor baby."

Allison's chin rested on Gina's shoulder, her face turned toward me. She closed her eyes and said, barely audible, "The worst part of all is, I really miss my mom." She started crying hard, the sobs coming out in big gulps.

"Oh, of course you do." Gina reached up and stroked her hair, the way she'd done for me a thousand times. And then I moved in to be part of it, and the three of us hugged and cried and talked and promised to keep in touch, until a man came in to tell us our time was up and we had to leave.

Chapter 36

Father's Day

Sitting in our parked car, I filled my mom in on the day Allison had tried to warn me about the other MHUCA kids. "I didn't know what she was trying to tell me, so I completely ignored her," I said. "Then those kids came running up to the fence swearing at me and scared the hell out of me."

"And she actually remembered you when she saw you in the lunchroom later?" Mom put her key in the ignition, but didn't start the engine. I guess neither of us was in a hurry to leave just yet.

"Yeah, that's what she said. Pretty amazing that she was able to pick me out of the crowd." Really amazing, if I thought about it. All I'd done was walk past a fence and laugh at a boy in the cafeteria, and because of those two things I wound up saving a girl's life. You never really know what a difference you can make in someone's life, if you're willing to let them in.

"I almost lost it when she said she missed her mom," Gina said. "I mean, you know Grandma and I don't see eye to eye, but still, at least I know she cares." This was a first. The beginning of a reconciliation maybe? No, probably not. "I can't imagine what Allison's going through, not having a mom at her age."

"Yeah, that has to be hard. Almost as bad as not ever having a father. Or even knowing who he is."

She looked pained. "Look, Rae, if I tell you, can we be done with this topic? Forever?"

I was startled. After being put off for so many years, I hadn't been expecting a straight answer. I said, "I just want to know the truth. His name, what he looked like, where he is." I looked at her straight on, and she met my eyes.

"Okay, this is the truth." She took a deep breath. "I don't know his last name or where he is. You'll never be able to find him, so get that out of your head right now. His first name was Ray. I met him when I was eighteen and working in a bar in Kansas City. He was a long-distance truck driver, and he used to come in all the time when he was in town. Sometimes we'd go out when I got off work. I went out with him three, four times, and then I never saw him again. By the time I realized I was pregnant, he was long gone. I tried to contact the trucking company he worked for, but they wouldn't give me any information. My guess is that he was married."

"You slept with some guy and didn't know his last name?"

She paused to get a cigarette out of the pack. "He told me his last name, I think. I just wasn't paying attention. It was a different time, Rae. The people I hung around with drank. A lot. And when you have drinking, you have casual sex. I'm older and wiser now, but that's the way it was. I wish I could tell you more, I really do." She rapped the pack against the dashboard until a cigarette slid out. "Over the years I hoped you'd stop asking. He's not here, I am, so I didn't think it made a difference."

"It makes a difference to me." I felt deflated. I'd always thought there'd be more to the story than this. A truck driver. How uninteresting was that? "What did he look like? Did he have any interests?"

She lit the Marlboro and inhaled. "Brown hair, nice features, medium build. His eyes were like yours. He liked sports. He was helpful."

"Helpful?"

"Yeah, like if someone at the bar needed their car jump-started, he was the first to offer to help. He left good tips for waitresses. When people looked sad, he tried to make them laugh." She looked thoughtful. "Ray was a nice man. He was maybe thirty when I knew him. I thought he was really old at the time."

"Do you have a picture? Anything?"

"What I just told you is all I have, Rae. If you want the name of the trucking company, I have it somewhere. You can try them again if you want, but sixteen years ago they weren't all that cooperative, and I can't imagine anything's changed." Mom pointed at me. "And don't you dare tell your grandparents. Their opinion of me is low enough already." She took a drag on her cigarette.

"Why wouldn't you tell me this before?"

She exhaled, the smoke coming out in a rush. "It's embarrassing, quite frankly. It makes me sound stupid, and I didn't want you to think of me that way. Besides," she added, smiling, "who needs him, right? The Maddox girls have always done fine on their own."

Chapter 37

The Real Rae Maddox Integration Program

I was still digesting this information when she started the engine and eased out of our parking space. I was now Rae, daughter of Gina and Ray—Ray's location unknown. I wondered if he still drove a truck. He could have logged millions of miles by now. He could be anywhere.

Had we been chasing him my whole life? I wondered if on some subconscious level mom was looking for him everywhere we went. We were traveling while he was traveling. We probably kept passing each other unawares, like in the movies where two people miss each other going in and out of side-by-side elevators. One of us really needed to stay put.

"Where to now?" Mom asked, interrupting my thoughts. "I don't have to work until three. You want to get something to eat?"

"No, I better get back to school." I pulled down the visor and checked myself out in the mirror. With all the crying, I was going to need a major eyeliner touch-up before I went back to class. "I have a big test seventh hour. I don't want to miss it."

Gina laughed. "You have the option of skipping school and you're *choosing* to go back? I would never have done that."

"Well, we're not exactly the same person, are we?"

When we got to school, I asked Mom to come inside to sign me in. Technically this wasn't necessary—high schools are more worried about kids leaving than sneaking back in—but she didn't know that.

In the office the usual lady was at work behind the counter, tapping away at her computer. What she was typing in there, I couldn't tell you. I had a theory that the office ladies spent the day shopping online and forwarding teacher jokes to friends, but I couldn't prove it.

She looked up when the door closed behind us. "Hello, Rae, what can I do for you?"

"I just returned from an appointment. My mom came to sign me back in."

Office Lady looked a little befuddled. "You don't need to do that if we have you down for an excused absence. You can just go on to your class."

"I was also wondering if Mr. Smedley is in his office. I'd like him to meet my mother." While she picked up the phone to check with the Smedster, Mom raised her eyebrows questioningly. I whispered, "He's the vice principal, the one that paired me with Allison."

After permission was granted, the office lady directed us down the hall. Mr. Smedley stood when we entered the room. I saw in his eyes the same look I always saw when men met my mother for the first time. I was betting he was thinking she was really cute (or hot, if he was that kind of guy, and really all guys are that kind of guy) and also that she looked too young to have a daughter in high school.

"Rae," he said, "how nice to see you. And this is your mother?"

I made the introductions, and he motioned for us to sit. Mom and I gave him the update on Allison. Some of it he knew already, some he didn't, but as we talked I could tell from his face that he really cared about Allison. He almost got teary when Gina told how Allison said she missed her mom, and I don't think it was just because my mom was emotional herself. Here I'd thought he was the usual all-business school administrator, but underneath that white shirt and striped tie was a real beating heart. Who knew? People surprise you sometimes.

"Mr. Smedley, there was something else I wanted to talk about as long as we're here," I said. "I know the Rae Maddox Integration Program was just an idea you were trying out, but I think it's a good one. Going to a new school is really stressful; no one knows that better than me. We've moved a lot over the years. More than a lot, really, an unbelievable amount, like nearly every year. Lucky for me, my mom promised we'd stay here until I graduate so I'd finally have that stability." I shot a glance in her direction and smiled. She looked a little startled, but she didn't look mad. Yet.

I took a deep breath and continued. "So I will be here for sure for the next two and a half years, and I'd like to accept your offer to be in charge of the Integration Program. I think I'd be good at matching students with the new kids. I have a lot of ideas, too. I thought the tech department could create a virtual tour. Maybe we could put it on the school's website."

He leaned forward and nodded, a thoughtful look on his face.

"I thought I'd write up explanations for things that are confusing when you're new, like how the lunch program works and things like that. I have a lot of other thoughts too that we can discuss, when we get the ball rolling. I'm actually pretty excited about taking on a leadership role for this program. That is, if you'll let me."

"It sounds like you've given this a lot of thought." He pushed his glasses up the bridge of his nose. I'd seen Mason do his Smed-ster impression many times using this exact same gesture, but suddenly it didn't look quite so funny. He turned to my mom. "Your daughter is really an outstanding girl, Ms. Maddox—good head on her shoulders, top-notch grades, compassionate toward her fellow students. I'm sure Allison would agree that she's a good friend to have too. You must be very proud of her."

"Yes, I am."

"Okay then." He leaned back and smiled at me. "The program is all yours. I'll set up a meeting with the guidance counselors, and we'll get together with them one day next week and hammer out the details. Deal?"

"Deal." We shook hands across the desk, me grinning like crazy, and my mom giving me this sly smile that could have gone either way.

After we'd said our good-byes to Mr. Smedley and were out of the office Gina said, "So we're not moving now for two and a half years?"

I had trouble reading her face. "I can't. I just made a commit-ment to run a new program. But if *you* want to move, Grandma and Grandpa said I could live with them and commute."

She sighed. "No way in hell. I'd rather live in this podunk town a while longer than give you up."

"Does this mean we're staying?"

"I guess. I did promise, didn't I?" She mimicked my own words right back to me. "So you'd finally have that stability."

I gave her a big hug right in the hallway of my high school, and I didn't even care who saw. "You really are the best mom in the world."

"Yeah, yeah, save it for another time." But she looked sort of pleased with herself. "You better get back to class, Rae. You don't want your GPA to suffer because your mother is a bad influence."

Chapter 38
Star Light, Star Bright

My cell phone rang at nine thirty, just as I finished going over my notes for a test in math, the last of my homework. I glanced at the caller ID. It was Nick. "Hey, I was just thinking about you," I said, which was true because he was always on my mind even when I was forced to think about other, less important things, like algebra.

"I'm parked in front of your building. Come on out."

I looked down at what I was wearing—a cami top and lounge-wear pants—and hesitated. "I'm in my pajamas."

"I don't care what you're wearing. Hurry up and get out here. I need an hour of your time. I have to show you something."

I threw on a sweatshirt, ran a brush through my hair, and put on socks and running shoes. It wasn't a good look, but what did he want on such short notice? I rushed past Gina in the kitchen gabbing on the phone to one of her salon friends. Talking them through a crisis, no doubt. I threw her an explanation as I went past. "Nick's outside. He wants to show me something. I'll be back in an hour."

"On a school night?" she asked in mock horror, then waved and turned back to her conversation.

Nick was mysterious about where he was taking me. He had a sneaky smile the whole time I was asking questions. Finally he said, "It's not a gift. It's just something I want to share with you."

When we arrived at his house, he parked alongside the barn and motioned for me to get out. Unlatching the tailgate, he helped me climb up into the back of the truck. I settled down and sat cross-legged on a comforter lining the bottom. "Look at this," he said, pulling a stack of blankets out of a box behind us. "I even brought the warmth." He wrapped a fleece blanket around my shoulders and went back to the box for a large stainless thermos and a mug. "And something hot to drink. Unfortunately, I only grabbed one mug, so we'll have to share." He unscrewed the top and poured. In the dark, the aroma of hot cocoa was especially strong. "Sorry I don't have whipped cream." He handed me the cup, which I took gratefully.

I sipped slowly, savoring the rich chocolate flavor. "This is so good. Did you make it?"

"All by myself."

I handed the mug back to him, and he took a swallow. "So where is the thing you wanted to show me?" I asked.

He reached over and lifted my chin with one finger. "Look up." I cast my gaze upward and saw the night sky like I'd never seen it before. The stars were beams of light shining through a pitch-black backdrop. I felt a surge of joy and wondered if this was how astronauts felt when they saw it from up there. "Oh, it's so beautiful."

"When it's not cloudy, you can really see the stars out in the country. Tonight it's as clear as it gets. When I saw the sky tonight I thought, *Rae has to see this*."

From behind us the back door of the house creaked open. Mrs. Dunstan called out, "Nicky, is that you?"

"Yeah, Ma, I'm looking at the stars with Rae."

"Well, don't stay out too long. It's getting cold."

"It's okay, Ma. Rae's wearing her warmest pajamas."

A slight pause. "Okay, dear." And then the sound of the door closing firmly as she went back inside. We both burst out laughing.

"She kills me," he said, shaking his head. "Now where were we? Oh yes." He put his arm around me and pulled me close. "The stars. Over there," he pointed, "you can see the Big Dipper and the Little Dipper. And my favorite star—"

"You have a favorite?"

"Oh yes, I do. And that would be the North Star. It's the last star in the handle of the Little Dipper. Sailors used to use it for navigation. Back then, if you could locate the North Star you could always find your way home."

"That's good to know."

We sat nestled together, drinking our hot chocolate for thirty minutes or maybe an hour. Time didn't matter. I could have sat there all night looking at the stars and breathing in the cool night air with Nick by my side. Finally I'd found my way home.

THE END

About the Author

Karen McQuestion has had literary aspirations since the third grade, when her teacher read her short story out loud to the rest of the class as an example of a job well done. She has been writing ever since. She lives in Hartland, Wisconsin, with her husband and their three children.

Made in the USA
San Bernardino, CA
16 November 2018